Amish Vows:

Amish

Princess

By Rose Doss

Book 2

Cover images courtesy of period images and canstockphoto
Cover by Joleene Naylor.

Manufactured/Produced in the United States

CHAPTER ONE

"Who is the pretty blonde girl sitting next to Martha Yoder? You know, Bishop Yoder's *Frau*." Isaac Miller asked his brother, Enoch, who sat in a chair beside him. Around them, the Amish Mannheim, Pennsylvania community chattered before the meeting started.

The Schwartz house grew warm as more families filed in for the worship service and the occasional woodsy puffs of smoke from the fireplace didn't help. Windows open to let in cool early spring breezes sent *Kapp* strings and beards fluttering as the hum of chatter filled the room, but probably also added to the gusts of acrid heat from the small fire. Rows of mismatched, serviceable chairs were filling as the noise of visiting neighbors rose around them.

A smirky smile eased onto Enoch's face. "You can see— under her black *Kapp*—that her hair is blonde?"

Rolling his eyes, Isaac admitted with a grin, "Of course. Do you know who she is or not? We can see by the dark *Kapp* that she's not married."

Leaning forward to look around her husband, Kate hissed, "She's the Yoder *princess*."

She managed to do this, holding baby Elizabeth over her shoulder and patting for a burb.

"What!? Princess?" Isaac yelped quietly. In their world, they believed themselves to be called by *Gott* to live simple lives of faith, dedication and humility. The Amish didn't believe in self-glory and even the idea of royalty was scorned. "The Yoder what?"

"You know," Kate said in a low voice, still patting the quietly-fussing *Boppli*, "Bishop Yoder's brother—the one living over at Elizabethtown—has five sons and only one daughter. Mercy. So they say she's been...coddled a bit. She's also the youngest of her family. Imagine a girl growing up with *five* protective big brothers?"

Flashing a glance at the pretty young woman sitting next to Martha Yoder, Isaac found himself asking his sister-in-law, "Why does she look so sad?"

Kate shrugged. "It is said that the *Mann* she was to marry—within weeks, mind you—ran away. Left the faith and disappeared into the *Englischer* world."

Blowing a soft puff of air through pursed lips, Isaac sat back. "That would trouble a girl."

"Do you two mind?" Enoch inserted his sardonic question from the chair between theirs, his eyebrows lifted.

Seeming unfazed, Kate shifted the *Boppli* to her other shoulder as she turned from her husband's admonishment to greet Samuel Miller, Isaac and Enoch's father who'd seated himself on her other side in the crowded room. "Welcome, *Daed* Miller!"

Even though Samuel was the father of six grown children and a widower, he was still strong and upright although going gray at his temples and his long beard held streaks of silver.

Isaac grinned a greeting at his *Daed* around Enoch and Kate.

"Good afternoon, *Dochder*." Samuel smiled back, leaning forward to tickle little Elizabeth's cheek. "It was too hot over with Lizzie and James, so I came to sit with you."

Ignoring the reference to his sister, Enoch again admonished them in a husky whisper to be quiet as Bishop Yoder stood in front of the congregation to offer the initial sermon. Bishop Yoder would yield later to Bishop King who would give the main sermon for the day.

Throughout the sermons, Isaac ignored his brother's occasional chin scratches—Enoch's beard was still growing in

2

although he'd married Kate over a year ago. It was only natural, Isaac told himself, that his gaze occasionally strayed to where Mercy Yoder sat several rows in front of him. For a Yoder woman, she was remarkably attractive. Even with her black *Kapp* pinned in place, he could see the smooth wings of her blonde hair and the fine texture of her skin.

In a booming voice, the broad Bishop Yoder spoke of the belief that *Gott* decided their eternal end by weighing individuals' lifelong obedience to His rules against their disobedience. He thundered at moments and spoke his words quietly at others, his face stern above his gray beard.

Settled back in his chair to listen, Isaac idly glanced around the community of worshipers who rustled quietly as they also attended the *Mann* preaching. Even if Bishop Yoder did harbor ill thoughts against Isaac's family—since Kate had chosen to marry Enoch, rather than the Bishop's then-adolescent son, Aaron—he still had a strong message to share.

In the few moments between the first speaker and the second, Isaac asked his brother, "Where's Sarah?"

"Over with the other girls." Enoch nodded toward the area where a cluster of girls huddled on chairs, giggles erupting now that the speaker had stepped down.

"Silly *Maedel*," he said in a fond voice.

Ezekiel Schmidt stood to speak then and they fell silent again, giving him their attention.

When this sermon was finished nearly an hour later and several songs had been sung in the usual High German, Kate handed still-fussing *Boppli* to Enoch, probably preparing to go help the other women in the kitchen. Isaac knew feeding everyone was an enormous task often done in shifts, but Kate loved cooking, so this was no chore to her.

Just then *Frau* Hochstetler stopped by, her girth blocking the breeze from the window as she said in a dramatic under voice, *"Goedemorgen.* Have you seen the Yoder girl up there, sitting by Martha?"

"Yah," Kate responded without enthusiasm.

"I have," Isaac said, looking back at beautiful Mercy Yoder with her blonde hair. He couldn't be sure from this angle, but he'd bet she had blue eyes, too.

"She's very pretty," the older woman said, her pale plump mouth primming, "but I hear the *Mann* she was to marry left his family in Elizabethtown and her—renouncing the church which he'd already joined—shortly before they were to say their vows. Just up and left. What can this say about her? No one knows why he left, but it can't help reflect on the Yoder girl. They call her the *princess* because she's had all these older brothers looking after her. And her parents, too. After five boys, the Yoders didn't think they'd have a *Dochder*."

Isaac felt himself turn to stone as he realized just who Mercy Yoder was… Who she had to be…and who she'd been betrothed to marry. Daniel Stoltzfus. She'd been preparing to marry Daniel. Why hadn't he realized this immediately when Kate had said who she was?

"I imagine not. I'm sorry, *Frau* Hochstetler, but I have to go help in the kitchen." His sister-in-law edged a little away from the woman.

Even though he was wrestling with his sense of guilt, Isaac watched with amusement as Kate tried to stem the garrulous woman's gossipy words.

"Of course! Of course. They say that the Yoder girl is to stay here with her uncle, Bishop Yoder, all summer. She gathers *wildflowers,* I've heard." This last was said with a repressive grimace, as though Rachel Hochstetler had something against wild blossoms. "She's supposed to make medicinal salves and potions from weeds and things. I don't know."

Her white *Kapp* pinned firmly enough not to move with the headshaking, the older woman rolled her eyes in emphasis.

Clearly trying to help his wife in an awkward moment, Enoch said, "That must be a blessing to some, if they are medicinal salves."

"*Yah,*" Rachel shrugged expressively. "She must do something to fill her hours, since she has no husband. I suppose *Gott* brings us every one to the right mate. At least, that what's said."

"Very true," Isaac responded with a grin.

"I must get to the kitchen," Kate tried again. "Excuse me, *Frau* Hochstetler."

"Of course. Of course." Rachel Hochstetler finally moved forward down the row.

"Well, *Bruder,*" Enoch turned to Isaac, jiggling the *Boppli*, "do you suppose this blonde Mercy Yoder is meant to marry Aaron?"

"You mean after Kate chose you instead? *Neh,* they are first cousins." Isaac slapped a goofy grin on his face, slipping automatically into his customary light-hearted banter.

Mercy Yoder had definitely been Daniel Stoltzfus' fiancée. In his unspoken shame, Isaac could only hope no one remembered that Daniel had spent several months in Mannheim at the Glick farm last year. Had Daniel told anyone what had led up to his leaving the Amish world? Surely not.

"It wouldn't be the first time cousins in our faith married." Enoch's mouth thinned. "Besides Aaron was too young for Kate. You know that."

Isaac elbowed his elder brother. "And she was still in love with you. Why else would she have asked you to marry her after her *Mamm* and *Daed* were killed in that buggy accident?"

Enoch smiled, looking very satisfied. "Bishop Yoder was still upset she didn't marry Aaron…even though he later counseled me to marry her."

"True, although it was his business as Bishop to help her work out what she'd do when widowed and alone after the deaths of her parents." Isaac laughed, throwing a glance at where the still-unmarried Aaron Yoder sat with several other young men. "Still, the Yoders have been frosty with the whole Miller family since then."

"That should put a crimp in your getting to know Mercy Yoder better," said Enoch with a dry smile.

Isaac leaned forward, his elbows on his knees. His gaze fell on the pretty girl sitting next to Martha. He felt a perverse desire—given his part in her situation—to get to know Mercy better. She was a beautiful woman, even when so sad. "It'll just make things more interesting."

"Not so much if this girl, Mercy, is meant to marry Aaron Yoder."

"Even if they weren't first cousins," Isaac cocked an eyebrow at his brother as he stood and turned toward the tables that had been set out for everyone to eat, "I'd still take my chances."

Later joining the stream of worshipers making their way to the tables that had been crowded into the house, he shifted and inched forward. As worship services were held in member homes, the rooms were packed with the faithful. A constant stream moved still through the narrow aisle between chairs as people jockeyed for places for the first sitting.

Isaac noted that as Zachariah Graber moved through the throng, he didn't look up or greet anyone, his face grim as usual. The old *Mann's Frau* had passed several years before and, his gray beard bristling angrily, he seemed to grow smaller and smaller with every day.

"Hello, *Frau*," Holding his straw hat loosely between his fingers as he passed by, Isaac bent to brush the other hand over the small boy's head. "Hello, little Abraham. Did you eat already?"

The tow-headed boy nodded vigorously as his mother said, "*Yah.* We're joining his *Daed* outside."

"*Gut.*" Isaac nodded, as the woman passed by, her belly swollen with Abraham's brother or sister.

Walking into the room where tables had been set up, he looked to find himself a place to sit, now that the little ones had been fed. The room was growing warmer still with the press of people and the kitchen at the other side.

Continuing to thread his way through crowd, Isaac suddenly found himself looking into the blue eyes of Mercy Yoder. He'd been right. Her eyes were a beautiful blue, like the summer sky.

Standing face-to-face with the girl teasingly called an Amish *princess*, Isaac found a smile sliding onto his face.

The crowd of people shifted around them as one group moved from the tables and another took their places.

In the jostling transition several *youngies* brushed against black-*Kapped* Mercy Yoder and—thrown off balance momentarily—she leaned into Isaac.

He caught the rounded, feminine armful, a fresh, flowery scent filling his indrawn breath. How could Daniel Stoltzfus have left such a comely bride? No matter what had been said to him.

She glanced up at him, her summer-blue eyes startled. Snapping at him in a flustered way, she straightened herself. "Can you not watch where you're going?"

"I'm sorry," Isaac said, setting her back on her feet. "But the house is crowded and the *youngies* meant nothing."

"They should watch where they're going," Mercy said, starting to move away. "They could have knocked me to the floor!"

Isaac couldn't help grinning. "Then I'd have had to haul you from the floor. Not such a great distance...and thankfully you're not of an age to break a hip."

She brushed her skirt. "That's no excuse to rush past so carelessly."

Hurrying into speech as she turned away, he commented. "I saw you sitting next to *Frau* Yoder in the meeting earlier. That must mean you are the Yoders' niece. I heard you're here for the summer."

The blonde girl swung her blue gaze back to him, a faint, scornful smile playing around the corners of her mouth. Her brows lifted. "Because I sat beside her, I must be the niece?"

"Yes." His reply was swift as he grinned back at her. "We are a small town, here in Mannheim. I'm Isaac Miller and I've always liked the name Mercy."

With a tantalizing glimmer of a polite smile, she inclined her head, saying, "*Goedemiddag*, Isaac Miller."

With that, pretty Mercy Yoder turned and disappeared into the throng.

He watched her go, admiring her sassy response. This could be fun…even if he did feel a little guilty.

The next day, Mercy stroked her hand over the smooth, red, lance-shaped leaves of Lady's Thumb as a bright blue sky smiled overhead. A fresh late-spring breeze brushed tall field grass against her faded green dress. In her mind, she catalogued all the plant's benefits, remembering what her *Grossmammi* had taught her. *Heart ailments. Stomachaches and sore throats.* Gathering several leaves, she laid them flat in her basket. Today was less windy than the day before, bringing a more gentle movement to the grass swaying around her. She'd always loved wandering through the fields with her *Grossmammi*, the old woman filled with wisdom about treating health problems naturally. *Englisch* doctors were costly and often not found nearby. Using what was given by *Gott* to treat illnesses benefitted all.

To her surprise, Mercy suddenly noticed an elderly *Mann* had entered the field only yards from where she stood. Pausing to exchange a polite greeting, she stopped only to see him walk past, as if she weren't there. Hunched a little, he never turned his gray head or looked up from the path in front of him.

Mercy watched him as he walked to the edge of the field and left it through a break in some tree branches. He'd moved passed her as if he'd never seen her. Reflecting that the old *Mann* must have had a load on his mind since he hadn't noticed he wasn't alone, she continued on, occasionally bending to gather beneficial herbs.

As the youngest in her family, Mercy had spent a lot of time with the Yoder matriarch, deemed too young and fragile to work the farm. She could still remember her *Grossmammi* singing softly to her in Dutch as she went to sleep. As she'd gotten older, they'd crafted healing lotions and salves in their kitchen after Mercy's light work in the house and the home garden was done.

Pausing, Mercy sent up a prayer to *Gott*, thankful He'd taken her beloved *Grossmammi* into His arms after she'd left this world. She still missed the wise woman's words and comfort. If only *Grossmammi* Schwartz were here now to tell Mercy what to do, how to…move forward. How to survive the crushing mess around her.

She knew there were church members in Elizabethtown who'd thought too little was required of her, that hard work led individuals to live in *Gott's* way. They'd believed her pampered, and the remembrance of her whispered nickname—*princess*—bought a heated flush to her cheeks. Had Daniel seen her as a lightweight? Unable to do her part?

Had that been a part of why he'd left? The possibility troubled her.

After Daniel's defection—his choice to leave the life and leave her, too—she didn't know how to face everyone. She'd gone from feeling secure that her life was mapped out, safe and loved in the service of *Gott* and family…to having no aim. No purpose. No place.

Coming here to Mannheim to stay with *Onkle* and *Aenti* Yoder for the summer had been her parents' idea after dealing with the community curiosity and talk, a way to let the dust settle from Daniel's abandonment.

Mercy raised her chin a notch. There was no denying she felt stained by his actions, but she refused to let that define her. Even if she wondered how she'd not known he was that conflicted… How she'd missed any hint that the *Mann* she was courting and had planned to marry wasn't committed to this life.

Dusting her hands after crumbling a chunk of damp soil through her fingers, she stopped to lift her gaze to a puffy white formation of clouds above her. A brilliant blue above her, the sky seemed endless and Mercy suddenly wished she were a bird that could fly high above the land. The creatures of the sky didn't wonder if they were worthy, if they could meet the challenges of this world.

She didn't need anyone's pity, though. It wouldn't change anything and it caused hot embarrassment to crawl under her skin. What did Daniel's actions say about her and his dread of marriage to her? The question troubled her, but she certainly didn't need Levi, Caleb, Micah, Joseph or Elijah conspiring to find Daniel and *school* him. The Plain people valued a life lived *Gott's* way, a way of non-violence. Daniel might have left their world—and was now shunned for it—but that didn't mean her older brothers could twist his head off. They needed to recognize they couldn't protect her from desertion by the *Mann* she was to marry.

Picking a few more leaves to put in her basket, Mercy made mental note of the location, so she could come back if she needed. The cool breeze gently brushed the strings of her black *Kapp* against her neck. She'd attended the service with her *Onkle* and *Aenti* and prayed to *Gott*, but she felt…still tarnished.

It was as if, by leaving both her and the life they'd planned to share, Daniel had tilted her into this strange, uncertain place. As if she'd fallen short and failed at being a good wife before she even was one. Settling onto a stone in the glen, surrounded by stems of long prairie grass, she brought her knees up to her chin, the long skirt of her dress falling to her ankles.

Please, Gott. Help me find my way. Gott never abandoned his faithful.

It hadn't been her idea to spend the summer with *Aenti* and *Onkle* here in Mannheim, but her *Daed* had thought the time with his brother would spare her from hearing the whispers she knew were flying around their community. Even though she missed her family a lot, it was a relief not to feel the glances sent her way, both kind and curious.

And possibly—she thought of Isaac Miller's cheeky grin and broad shoulders as she'd walked away from him at the meeting— the summer might have some brighter spots.

A week later, Isaac brushed sawdust off the wood beneath his plane, before setting it again in motion. He loved the smell that rose from the wood he shaped.

"And what are you making this time," his *Daed* sat on a stool nearby, the woodshop windows thrown open to let in the late spring air.

"A bed. Hannah and John Hochstetler's little girl, Lydia, is ready for a bed of her own."

"Have they built onto the house? I didn't know they were expanding it or I'd have offered a hand. They already have four *Bopplis* in the one room." Samuel's brown hair was now heavily flecked with gray, but he could easily keep pace with his four sons when it came time to plow the fields or swing a hammer.

A light spring breeze wafted through the workshop.

"I think John's brothers pitched in. They said the frame didn't take more than a day." Isaac pushed the plane over the wood surface again, feeling the stretch of his muscles as he reached the length of the plank. This was all so familiar and soothing to him.

"Enoch and Kate said you were eying the pretty Yoder girl who is visiting Brother Hiram this summer. Do you think to win over even a Yoder female with your flirting?" His father's voice was indulgent.

Isaac pushed another curl of wood off the plank, letting a smile quirk the corner of his mouth. "Did they say that? Then maybe they were pulling your leg. You sat right there on the other side of Kate. If I was flirting, you'd have heard."

"She's a nice-looking girl," his father commented, a glimmer of Isaac's own teasing in his voice. "She might ignore her *Onkle's* warnings about us Millers, if you're sweet enough. Enough girls have, you *Schaviut*."

"I'm grown out of my rascal phase. And, *yah,* she is comely. No doubt about it." Isaac squelched a smile. After all the teasing he'd done, he had no right to squawk when it came back his way. "Say, didn't you tell me you were going over to see James and Gideon?"

The rich scent of freshly-planed wood mixed nicely with the scent of blooming fruit trees just outside his shop and Isaac paused a moment to enjoy taking a breath. "I miss James and Gideon. I wish they were closer. You should go visit to make sure they're courting nice *Maedels*."

His other two brothers had both bought farms in a town a hundred miles away, since they'd found them at a good price, and visits between the relatives had to be planned.

Samuel shifted on the stool, ignoring Isaac's comments about his brothers with a smile both gentle and gleeful. "You might see this Mercy Yoder at the Sing that Kate and Enoch will host. She might teach you that you can't win all girls. You're too cocky by half, in this area. You need to find one woman. Settle down, get married to a good wife and work more on your farm, like your *Bruders*. All this furniture building is one thing, but the land will never let you down. It is *Gott's* way."

"Yes, *Daed*," Isaac finally grinned at his father, lifting the now smooth plank to lean it against the wall amongst others. "I know."

"You're not getting any younger, *der Suh*." Samuel Miller commented. "You've already joined the church. It's time you married and started a family. Maybe that Mercy Yoder is the right woman for you. You should at least pick one."

"Yes, *Daed*. And it would go over big with her *Onkle* if I picked that one, I'm sure. You know how the Yoders feel about Kate choosing to marry Enoch rather than their *youngie,* Aaron Yoder."

"Yes, but that kind of thing has never stopped you before. If a girl is pretty." his father told him.

"Well, if you do want to go see James and Gideon—to check up on how they're doing," Isaac said with a cheeky grin as he returned to his earlier question, "Enoch and I can watch over your place."

"I'm seeing them in the fall." His father got off the stool, brushing a stray curl of wood off his leg. "You and Enoch have your own land to watch in the planting and harvesting time. In the fall, the fields will be fallow. You'll have time to watch my farm

12

and mess about with your wood. You can do both then. No reason to neglect your own farm."

Samuel stopped before exiting the workshop, throwing another smile toward Isaac. "I hope you have a good time at the Sing after this next service. You know, we Millers have never particularly cared about whether others like us or not."

As his father's footsteps receded, Isaac chuckled, continuing to shape the bed. The hush of the plane over wood had always been a peaceful sound to him. He didn't think he was neglecting his fields, but he did love this work. The timber seemed almost alive beneath his hands. Even as a *youngie*, still new to carpentry, he'd loved the smell of cut lumber, the solidness of the wood beneath his hands. He'd spent days in Abel Glick's wood workshop, learning all he could.

He smiled. Those had been good childhood days: the running wild in the afternoons after the trial of poring over his books. None had been more glad to have finished schooling when it was done. His *Geschwischder* had roamed the fields, too, as *youngies*, but none of his brothers and sisters had been as much an adventurous boy as himself. Isaac's mouth quirked as he remembered how *verrickt* he'd been. Wild and rambunctious and full of energy.

If only he'd learned to see all the consequences of his actions…

Pushing the plane again over the board in his hands, the smile fell from his face. His father was right. Mercy Yoder was a good-looking woman. He just wished he'd had no hand in her current situation. Wished he'd never met Daniel Stoltzfus.

That fall a year back, Mercy's fiancé had come to Mannheim to visit family—a relative of the same Abel Glick who'd taught Isaac so much in the past before he'd fallen ill. Isaac had readily worked old Abel's fields, never thinking of the outcome of his working alongside Daniel.

Isaac had never intended Daniel to take him seriously that teasing night. Not really. Never thought the *Mann* would find the spark in Isaac's jokey bantering to leave this Amish life… Not even when the joking had turned into jeering. Daniel was hard to work with, but that didn't excuse Isaac's sin.

Two days later the screen door of Bontreger's general store in Mannheim closed behind Mercy as she followed her *Aenti* Martha inside, her footsteps echoing on the wood floor. The store served their small community, supplying everything the plain, simple folk couldn't trade for or make themselves. Mercy smiled at and exchanged smiles with an exiting young *Frau* she'd met at the meeting, but whose name she couldn't remember.

As she walked through along the shelves, she felt soothed by the sense of familiarity around the place. There was a store just like this at home in Elizabethtown that smelled of lemon juice and vinegar and fresh produce brought in from the farms nearby. As she examined a small area stocked with home remedies, she trailed her hand along the smooth wood shelf, barely registering the few others in the store. Back at the counter, her *Aenti* chattered with the store owner and his *Frau,* her shopping basket on her arm.

Still examining the tonics and ointments in the small section, Mercy stepped forward to the shelf to let a *Maedel*—a girl child— walk by behind her, her steps loud on the wood floor boards. Shifting back to her original position once she could, Mercy made a face at the small shelf area. Basic items, mostly. And nothing for the many ailments necessary to a hard life of getting crops from the soil. Many times, she'd used *Grossmammi's* peppermint lavender balm to ease *Daed's* body aches and yet there was nothing like that here.

Knowing *Aenti* Martha had a long list of goods to get—not counting her tendency to lengthy chats—Mercy meandered down the aisle, almost able to pretend she was back at home. She missed her own little town. Before Daniel's defection had laid her open to both the pity and censure of neighbors, home had been such a peaceful, loving place. It had never made any sense that she was somehow responsible for his choice, but still…

She wondered—and she knew others did as well—had she somehow caused him to leave?

At the end of a shelving row of pickled beets, rich red in their jars, Mercy saw an attractive beardless *Mann* standing at a closed door off to the side of the building, his shirt sleeves rolled up to show brown, muscled arms.

Isaac Miller.

"Sarah," he said to the closed door, in an urgent undervoice. "I can't hear you, *Liebling*. Open the door. Are you crying?"

Unmoving, Mercy watched him.

"*Bencil*. Sarah let me in." He leaned closer to the door, dropping his voice. "Are you alright? Why can't you come out of the restroom?"

All of a sudden, Mercy realized that the girl who'd walked past her must be the one now inside the restroom. She looked around the store to see if she could find the child's mother and alert her to the *Bencil* having a problem. The child might be sick.

The owners stood at the front counter, talking still to *Aenti* Martha, but the only other two women she could see—one over by the produce and one at the pickle barrel—were clearly too old to be the child's *Mamm*. A *Grossmammi* perhaps? There was no way to know and the *Maedel* was obviously upset about whatever problem she had.

Moving forward, Mercy stopped next to Isaac, peripherally aware that he was even more attractive than she remembered and smelled nicely of clean air and fresh wood. She had no idea who the child was to him, but she felt compelled to offer help.

"*Goedenmorgen*, Isaac Miller. May I be of help?"

Whipping his head around, a harassed look on his face, he said, "Oh. Oh, *yah*. Sarah, *Liebling*, a nice lady is here. A friend of mine. Will you talk to her? Tell her the problem?"

Blinking at her quick elevation to friendship, Mercy waited in silence, standing next to him by the door.

"You can't get my *Mamm*?" It was a feeble question.

"*Liebling*, you know she's too far away."

Standing at his shoulder, Mercy registered the warmth of his nearness and refocused on the tearful, childish voice on the other side of the door.

"My *Bruder*, Enoch's daughter," Isaac whispered over his shoulder to Mercy. "She won't come out and I don't know why!"

There was no answer as the girl, apparently, thought about his offer.

"Well," a small voice wavered through the paneled wood door. "Okay, I guess."

The door lock could be heard being pulled back, before she eased the door open a crack.

"My *Mamm* told me this would happen," Sarah said several minutes later, as she sat glumly on the closed toilet seat. "I just didn't... It's just..."

"I know," Mercy responded with sympathy, pressing her hand against the girl's skirt-covered knee. She squatted against the wall in the small restroom, remembering her own transition to womanhood. "Even when you know what to expect, it can be a total shock the first time. Does your tummy hurt, too?"

"Yes." Sarah heaved a great sigh. "I thought I was sick or had eaten something bad."

"Is the pad I gave you comfortable? I only had a couple of handkerchiefs, but your *Mamm* will have plenty of cloths just for this."

"Yes. I guess it's okay." The girl blushed as if realizing she sounded ungracious. "Thank you, Mercy. I didn't know what to do. I just thought I needed to use the restroom and then there was all this..."

"It can be scary." Mercy smiled. "Like you're dying or something."

"And I'm here with my *Onkle* Isaac..." She drew a deep breath, turning pink. "I just couldn't come out of the restroom. It's just so embarrassing!"

Mercy straightened in the small restroom, saying with bracing encouragement. "You have nothing to be embarrassed about, Sarah. It's a very natural thing that every girl goes through. But, of course, it's very private. Don't worry about your *Onkle* Isaac. I'll make sure he doesn't bother you about this."

Getting up slowly, Sarah said, "You can do that? Thank you, Mercy."

Leaning against the wall near the door, Isaac idly staring ahead as he mused about a kitchen shelving unit he was making for *Frau* Glick, now that her husband was no longer with her. It was the least he could do since he'd originally learned woodcraft from old Abel Glick.

Isaac had heaved a sigh of relief when Mercy Yoder slipped into the restroom with Sarah. Kate and Enoch often trusted him with the *youngie*, particularly now that Kate's hands were filled with caring for the *Boppli*, as well as Sarah, Enoch and the house. He certainly didn't want to do anything to lose their trust.

Spending some time mentally measuring the various bottles and jars on the store shelves and making note, so he could accurately build the Glick's unit, he was aware of murmuring voices coming from the restroom. At least, Sarah sounded less hysterical now. The realization cheered him.

After a half hour or so, the door beside him opened.

Isaac straightened from the wall to see Mercy come through the restroom doorway, followed by Sarah, her cheeks pink and her little black-*Kapped* head down.

With her hand on the girl's shoulder, Mercy said, "Sarah, why don't you go out and wait in your *Onkle's* buggy. I'm sure he'll be out in a moment."

The child murmured something that could have been agreement, hurrying down the store aisle to the door.

Standing next to the beautiful blue-eyed woman, Isaac watched his niece disappear.

Turning toward him, Mercy said briefly, "Don't ask her anything, Isaac Miller. Nothing. Do You hear me?"

"What? Nothing? Why?" he responded, confused. "If the *Liebling* is sick, I need to tell her *Mamm* and *Daed*."

Walking with him towards the door, she said repressively, "Listen, Isaac. She's not sick. Don't even mention it to her. She'll tell her *Mamm* about it."

Mystified, he just shook his head.

She lowered her voice, giving him a significant look. "It's a *girl* thing. Don't mention it to her or she'll be terribly embarrassed."

"A girl thing?" Comprehension dawned. "Oh! A *girl* thing."

"*Yah*, a girl thing." Mercy repeated with emphasis as she waved at Sarah through the window, a reassuring smile on her face.

It hit Isaac all at once how embarrassing the incident would have been for the child and he reached out to shake Mercy's hand. "*Denki,* Mercy. You really helped. I won't say a thing. I'll act like it never happened."

"Good. See that you do. And goodbye." She turned to walk to where her *Aenti* Martha stood, still chatting at the counter.

He watched her walk away, reflecting on the fierce look she'd given him when she told him to say nothing to Sarah. So, the Amish princess had a kind heart? What would he have done without her?

It made him even more intrigued by the pretty woman…and guiltier about what he'd said to Daniel Stoltzfus.

CHAPTER TWO

"*Onkle* Hiram, I'm not looking for a husband now," Mercy repeated a week later, clinging to patience as she reminded herself that her uncle was only trying to help.

They sat at the table, the windows steamed by heat from a wood stove that crackled and sizzled in the corner, the smell of burning kindling filling the room.

"Listen, *Nibling*," her *Onkle* said, his long beard framing his face, "You must put that *Schlang* Daniel Stoltzfus behind you. This is the reason you came here to us in Mannheim. The only way to get past this is to find yourself another *Mann* to marry."

"*Yah.*" Martha Yoder agreed from her steamy spot by the kitchen stove, the scent of breakfast strong.

Mercy put up a hand to one of her warm cheeks. The room seemed closed-in and her relatives unhearing. A cow bell could be heard from outside and the sound brought to her the sudden image of a wide open field. It seemed incredibly tempting right now, even if it was chilly. Smoothing her cotton skirt, she struggled to keep the frown off her face.

She'd said all this to them so many times before.

Taking a breath to keep from speaking as hotly as she felt, Mercy said in a calm voice, "*Onkle* and *Aenti,* Daniel isn't a snake. I'm not sure what he is—other than mistaken—but I don't want a husband who doesn't want me...or one who isn't in our faith. I'm not still pining for Daniel."

"Of course," her *Onkle* Hiram agreed, "but this should be forgotten and nothing will help you more than having a home, a husband and a *Boppli* of your own."

"I know this. I have prayed about it and I hope that eventually *Gott* will send the right husband." Someone so strong in his choice of *Gott* and this life that she knew she could never drive him from his path.

"There is no doubt," *Aenti* Martha joined them at the table, smoothing her apron with a knotted hand, "that *Gott* will send the right *Mann*, Mercy. It will make his job not so difficult, however, if you'll let the right one close to you."

Onkle Hiram spooned the cooked cereal to his mouth before saying, "Your *Aenti* is right. *Gott* may have sent the one right here. You need to look around you. It won't do for you to fall in with another *Schlang*."

Feeling her lips press together, Mercy swallowed hard against the annoyance that rose in her and stirred the untasted cereal in front of her, the scent of cooked grains rising from it.

"Now take Aaron. He's a good *Mann*, able to provide for a strong family—"

"And while a very nice *Mann*, he's my first cousin!" She couldn't keep the tart note out of her voice. "I'm sorry. Forgive me."

She put down her spoon. "I'm afraid I'm not hungry, *Aenti*. May I be excused from the table? I believe I spotted some agrimony on my walk the other day. I'd like to go gather some. It's good for colds and fevers."

"Of course, Mercy. And you're welcome to use the kitchen to make any of your tonics." Her *Aenti* gave her a kind smile.

Mercy rose. "*Denki*. Excuse me, *Onkle*. I should be back to help with lunch."

"*Nibling*, you should consider the men here around us. Maybe *Gott* will have sent one of them," her *Onkle* recommended as she got up from the table. "Just be careful of the Millers. I think you could do better than them. The two other unmarried Millers live a ways from here, but you can definitely do better than that Isaac Miller."

"*Yah*," her *Aenti* chimed in. "Much better."

Mercy said nothing to this, her mouth firming as she held back heated words. They again hadn't heard anything she'd said. "I'll be back shortly."

"Go," her *Onkle* recommended. "Gather your herbs and think about what we've said."

Quickly gathering her basket, her snippers and a pair of smooth, worn leather gloves, she headed into the fields, still fuming as she walked through the swishing grass. If *Onkle* didn't have a miff with the Millers, she supposed he'd be throwing her at Isaac Miller, too. This pushing her into marriage made her furious. It wasn't just *Aenti* and *Onkle* Yoder, though, that kept bringing up this subject of her finding another *Mann* to marry.

A cool breeze fanned her cheeks as she walked, her arm threaded through the handle of her basket.

She was hounded about the matter everywhere she turned. In the letter she'd gotten only yesterday from her *Eldre*—tucked now into the bottom of her basket—had said almost the same thing. It was natural that her parents worried, but did they only see the one way through this mess?

Perhaps it was her. No one said anything about what she may or may not have done to push Daniel away, but she was very aware that this had most likely occurred to them, as well.

Tramping along the ground, the morning dew making her shoes damp, Mercy's basket dangled from her arm as thoughts played through her head. While it wasn't her choice, she'd been the youngest with five older brothers—a princess—she knew that reality was behind every word in the troubled letter they'd sent. Never spoken in their home, she realized her *Mamm* and *Daed* worried about that, thinking somehow she'd been spoiled and given too much and that this had scared Daniel from marrying her.

The fresh scents from grass and random wild flowers strewed throughout the pasture—both sharp and sweet—comforted her as she walked on. The stems of smartweeds and peppergrass brushed against her faded skirt and she felt comforted just being out in nature. The air smelled of wonderful growing things…mixed with the occasional whiffs of manure fertilizer.

Mercy carefully crossed the culvert between two fields—still filled with puddles from spring rains—walking on. The creaking croak sounds of hidden frogs following her.

Daniel's defection—both from her and from their faith—had left her scarred. Too much so to jump into marriage with anyone else, much less a *Mann* she hardly knew. No matter what they all said, she knew what they thought. It didn't do to say anything to anyone, but she couldn't shake the conviction that she'd somehow played a part in Daniel's defection. They'd courted several long years. She thought she'd known him.

Did others really think the idea of marriage to her had driven him from the life? It was strange to see judgment on the faces of those she'd known and loved her whole life. Friends she'd grown up with now treated her like she had a disease.

Scuffing her shoed feet against ground that was mossy in spots, she tramped along, wrestling with the fear that perhaps they were right. She'd prayed about it so many times. It didn't seem fair that she faced this. Mercy lifted her chin in momentary defiance. She hadn't chosen to be the only girl in her family, hadn't asked to be sheltered from work in the fields and cares around the farm. She'd even begged her *Mamm* for a baby brother or sister.

Even as a "princess", it seemed unlikely that she could drive Daniel to his horrendous actions, but there it was…

Stopping to carefully pick through a clump of prickly blackberry, Mercy drew out her small hand spade and loosened a white section of root from the base of the plant. She was glad of her gloves to avoid the plant's thorns, reflecting that when boiled it would add nicely to her treatments for mouth sores and gum inflammations. Her *Grossmammi* had always collected some.

Walking on to where she remembered the agrimony growing, she followed the path down to the trickling creek bed, the sound of even this small stream soothing as it burbled along. Balancing to extend a foot across the nearly-dry creek, Mercy spotted a black-coated figure some five or six yards down the creek bed, his broad hat sheltering his face. Sitting near a deeper pool of water, seeming to gaze into the pool was the elderly *Mann* she'd seen earlier when gathering herbs the other day. As before, he never looked up or gave any notice of her presence.

Mercy stepped across the stream and stood watching him, registering his gray hair and his lined face, seeming older because of the trouble there. It felt strange not to offer him a greeting. For some reason, his soul seemed troubled and she could felt she could understand that. There was no knowing what worry he contemplated so morosely, but she thought she recognized pain in his set, angry face.

Knowing better than to call out to him, she stood a moment watching him. As troubled as he seemed, he'd have nothing to say to a stranger.

Turning away from the creek bed, she climbed up to the next field, her mind returning to the matter of her *Onkle* and *Aenti's* actions, not to mention the silent implication from her *Mamm* and *Daed*.

Mercy sent up a prayer for patience to deal with the multiple people pushing her towards marriage with any eligible *Mann*…and even some who weren't so eligible. Like her cousin, Aaron. It was almost as if they truly did believe that Daniel's actions were somehow due to a lack in her and that she should marry quickly to put that to rest.

It was as if nothing would stop their pushing at her besides her courting with a *Mann*, pretty much any *Mann* besides Isaac Miller.

Stopping in the warmth of the sun, she sat on a stump, pulling the letter from her basket to read again. The sight of *Mamm's* handwriting made Mercy blink back sudden tears. She missed home…and her brothers and the deep rumble of *Daed's* voice. Growing up on the farm cherished in her family had been wonderful.

Even with being abandoned by Daniel, the world around her had been good and the thought that she might drive another to abandon a life with *Gott* was too horrifying to contemplate. But she couldn't tell anyone that was her fear. Not *Onkle* and *Aenti* or *Mamm* and *Daed*. It was too awful to even speak.

Several days later, Isaac hefted the hammer, feeling the weight of it in his hand. He brought it down, mindful of avoiding Enoch's hands. His *Bruder* held up new wiring that he and Isaac were stringing in place around Isaac's new chicken coop. With a few ringing thumps, Isaac secured the wire sheet in place, making swift work of the job.

Spitting the leftover u-shaped wire nails into his hand, Isaac cocked his head toward his brother as the metallic taste faded. "Is *Daed* coming to the Sing at your house?"

Around them, the farm yard crackled with the sounds. The jingling of the harness on Enoch's buggy horse's head mixed with the sound of distant mooing from a pasture over the ridge and, above in the trees, bird could be heard in their spring-time excitement.

"Now why would *Daed* do that?" Enoch stretched the wire around another side of the coop. "Sings are meant for *youngies* looking to find suitable partners."

"Because Kate is cooking for this Sing—and he's probably tired of his own—and don't you think it's time he found a new *Frau*? He's not a *youngie*, but he's not dead. He still has years of living ahead of himself. There should be some older women at the Sing. *Mamm's* been gone for years and *Daed's* been alone too long." Isaac pulled to tighten the wire mesh.

Enoch braced the wire against the corner two-by-fours. "You can ask him yourself about the Sing since he's coming to help us this morning. He said he'd like to roof something smaller than a house or a barn. I think he just likes to help...and James and Gideon's farms are too far away to be able to help much."

Muscling the wire netting around another corner of the coop, Isaac made a face. "Yes, *Daed* said he was coming to help with the coop. He's lonely since *Mamm* died. I'm telling you, he needs to remarry."

Enoch waited to respond until Isaac swiftly tacked the wire mesh against the corner board with wire nails he fished from his palm. "You know who needs to marry? You. And by the way, the Yoder princess will be at the Sing. You know, the blue-eyed, blonde-haired one? The girl who helped you at the Bontreger's store when Sarah locked herself in the restroom?"

"*Yah*, I remember," Isaac grinned. "Thank *Gott* she was there. That Mercy Yoder is certainly sassy from my brief dealing with her. Don't you think I ought to try to make friends with her? Just to needle Bishop Yoder, if nothing else?"

A smile broke out on Enoch's face just as their father's buggy trotted into sight, slight puffs of dirt rising with the horse's hooves. "I think you are looking for trouble, you flirt, and I suspect that Mercy Yoder might be the one to give it to you. Not to mention the bishop and his son."

"Hallo!" Samuel Miller called from his buggy. "Oh, I see you've made good progress. Let me stable Barley and I'll come help."

"Sounds good," Isaac called before turning back to his nailing. He cocked an eyebrow at his brother. "And if getting to know girls means I'm a flirt, then I learned from you. How long was it between Kate's marrying the first time and her asking you to marry? The *Eldre* despaired for you in those years."

"*Mamm* and *Daed* knew why I didn't look at other girls seriously." Enoch shifted to pull the wire around the next corner of the chicken coop.

Ignoring his stoic brother's lack of expression, Isaac grinned again. "You mean they knew you were still in love with Kate from when you two were *youngies*? What would you have done if Jakob Bieler hadn't died and left Kate a widow?"

"*Gott* would have provided. I'm sure he'd have sent me another bride." Enoch shifted his hold on the wire.

Throwing him a glance, Isaac said, "But it's hard to imagine loving any other woman the way you love Kate."

"*Yah.* I'm just grateful it didn't come to that and I got a *wunderbarr Dochder* in the bargain." A smile creased Enoch's normally serious face. "Sarah's a peach."

Smiling back at him, Isaac nodded. "And she's becoming a woman already. I was never more relieved than when Mercy Yoder helped me at the store. Poor Sarah! How embarrassing to have to tell your *Onkle* a thing like that!"

"Kate and I were glad she was there to help, too." His brother pulled the wire mesh around the final corner. "Maybe you should flirt with Mercy a little, just to break up her Yoder exposure."

"Maybe I could be of some help in that way, after what she did for me," Isaac agreed.

CHAPTER THREE

"Mercy, this is Abraham Schwartz." Her *Onkle* smiled broadly at the meeting held at the Miller home several days later.

Hoping her smile didn't look as insincere as she felt, Mercy let the sweaty older *Mann* take her hand. She had no doubt as to why this specific introduction was being made.

"Nice to meet you, Mercy Yoder." The *Mann* in front of her said awkwardly after he shook her hand, his wide straw hat clutched in large rawboned hands, his full beard proclaiming his age as much as the lines on his face. Tall and broad, he smiled and nodded as if he didn't know what else to say.

"Nice to meet you, too." Mercy again forced a medium-sized smile onto her lips as she stepped aside to allow a woman carrying a *Boppli* to pass. Behind them, the mass of church folk conversed and the sound rose in a small roar, making conversation difficult as the sound of chatting bounced off the walls.

Even in with the coolness of spring outside, it was close and warm in here. Accustomed to the smell of warm bodies massed together for worship, the smell almost signaled Sunday to Mercy.

The main room of the Miller home wasn't near big enough to hold everyone and seats had been set up not only in adjoining rooms, but also a row lined the hallway and some were outside the open windows. The main room was packed with chairs and since the aisles between these were narrow, it was hard to find a place to stand. Her *Onkle* Yoder managed, however.

"Abe here has a very nice farm—"

Smiling and nodding, she shifted to the side again as several others passed, flushing with awareness that Isaac Miller was with them.

"—and his three daughters keep the house and manage the garden very well while his four sons work the fields with him." *Onkle* beamed and nodded, his expression becoming appropriately solemn when he said, "Abe's *Frau* died in child birth several years ago."

With effort Mercy kept the pleasant expression on her face while conveying sympathy. This continued presentation by *Onkle* and *Aenti* of every possible mate was getting annoying, not to mention embarrassing. She only hoped Isaac hadn't realized what her *Onkle* was trying to do. Not wanting to seem unfriendly, she said again to the perspiring farmer, "It's very nice to meet you, Abe Schwarz."

The older man nodded again, the awkward smile still stretching his face. "*Yah.*"

As another family and the same grim-faced elderly man she'd seen before squeezed past them, *Onkle* Yoder patted the large farmer on the shoulder in dismissal. "Well, you two can talk later, I suppose."

As Abe moved away to find a seat, Mercy whispered, "*Onkle*, you and *Aenti* must stop this!"

"Stop what, *Nibling*?" An innocent, questioning expression slipped onto his face.

Hissing in an under voice as she shifted again to the side, Mercy said, "Introducing me to all these *Menner*! This Abe Schwartz is the third today. Not to mention the others you and *Aenti* have placed in my path in the last few weeks!"

She could feel herself blushing, knowing that Isaac and his brother, Enoch, sat nearby with *Bobbli* Elizabeth on his knee.

"Come, my *Nibling*." Seeming unaware that they were being observed, her *Onkle* clasped her by the elbow with thick fingers as he moved sideways through the group. "Your *Aenti* is saving a seat for you over here."

"*Onkle* Yoder!" She repeated, side-stepping through the noisy, crowded room after him, "Did you hear me?"

He stopped. "Of course, Mercy. But you know what your *Aenti* and I believe. There are good *Menner* here. You can find someone better than that *Schlang*, Daniel."

She opened her mouth to softly protest yet again when he interrupted.

"Just don't trust Isaac Miller. That Miller family—" He sent a darting glance toward where Isaac and Enoch sat, shaking his head with a frown descending onto his face. "It is not our place to question the faithfulness of others, but the Millers aren't the best match for you. Why Kate Bieler wanted that Enoch Miller, instead of your cousin, Aaron, I cannot understand. Of course, the other two Miller *Bruders* live several counties away now, but still. Isaac Miller is not for you."

"*Onkle* Yoder!" Mercy felt herself growing hot. "*Shush*! They might hear you!"

Finished his condemnation of the Millers, the older man made no response and started sidestepping again through the crowded room. Mercy followed after, catching up to him to lean forward and hiss. "I told you and *Aenti* that I don't mean to marry anyone immediately! I'm not looking for another *Mann*!"

Her *Onkle* pulled down the corners of his mouth, leaning toward her to say in a barely audible voice, "And this is where you're wrong, Mercy. You must let *Gott* lead you to another mate. Let those with more age and wisdom guide you. Now, over there. Your *Aenti* has a seat for you."

As her *Onkle* turned to go to his place in the front to speak, Mercy looked after him with growing frustration. Apparently the older and wiser believe *Gott's* wishes were in line with their own and weren't concerned about listening to her requests in this.

As well as being warm, the house was so full, Mercy had to step past several others to slide into the row with her *Aenti* and she saw again that same elderly *Mann* she'd seen in the fields—still angry-looking—still staring ahead as if no one was around him.

Several rows behind and to the side, her cousin Aaron sat with several other young *Menner*, not apparently fazed by the service being held in Enoch and Kate's house that day. Mercy liked Aaron. Not appearing at all wounded by Kate's choice to marry Enoch instead of him, Aaron talked and kidded with his friends. He'd grown up a lot in the last year and she hoped *Onkle* and *Aenti* would allow him, at least, to find his own mate.

Eventually sitting next to *Aenti* Yoder in the saved chair, Mercy began fanning herself slowly as the room grew warmer and she felt her heart rate settle down. The sermons today spoke of *Gott's* grace and the importance of trusting him. Mercy listened attentively, letting none of her confusion about her own situation show on her face. The community didn't need to be included in this any more than it already was, particularly if Isaac was watching. She couldn't understand why Daniel had left the church and she'd come to realize that his action was between him and *Gott*—even though others, and sometimes herself, believed she was at fault. He hadn't said much to her the last time they'd spoken in Elizabethtown, where they had grown up. Only that he couldn't marry her and needed to make his own way in the world. The *Englisch* world. His leave-taking of her had seemed almost unthinking, as if it was just part of his bigger decision to leave the Amish life. As if she were an add-on or something. It should have made her feel better about not missing him that much now that he'd left, but she still felt bad about this.

Before he went, Daniel garbled out something about being strong and not needing to be sheltered.

Mercy hadn't been able to make sense of it then and she couldn't still, but as she contemplated the speaker at the front of the gathering, she admitted to herself, moving her paper fan gently, that in the last few weeks, she hadn't so much missed Daniel as the life with him she'd thought was ahead of her.

This was a startling realization, but the thought had come to her over and over.

There were unmarried Amish women, of course, but she'd never thought she'd find herself amongst them. Never thought before that she'd end of up a childless, husband-less woman.

Maybe she'd just fallen in with Daniel out of familiarity. Every time that possibility occurred to her, Mercy shuddered. Certainly, *Gott* wanted better for her.

If *Onkle* and *Aenti* had their way, she'd marry some *Mann*—apparently any *Mann* except Isaac Miller—regardless of whether she and her husband suited. In the last few tumultuous weeks, however, Mercy had slowly come to the realization that she didn't want just any *Mann*. And that maybe she'd settled for Daniel because he'd been there and been interested in marrying her.

She didn't think it was in *Gott's* plan for her to settle for just any husband. He wanted his children happy and flourishing. Mercy felt her jaw firming.

Off to the side of the crowded room, she saw Hannah and her husband, John Hochstetler, and their brood of children. Mercy smiled back when she realized Hannah was nodding and smiling at her. Sitting here in the meeting, Mercy missed home and her family so much it felt like parts of her were breaking inside. It was nice to have made friends like Kate and Hannah and young Anna Lehman, Kate's cousin.

Making new friends didn't take away the piercing sense of missing her own family and all her brothers, but it did help. If Levi, Caleb, Micah, Joseph and Elijah knew how miserable she felt here without them all—as well as Joseph's wife and children—she knew her brothers would ride to bring her home to Elizabethtown. Not that all had been peachy for her there. Her *Mamm* and *Daed* were probably right. She needed a change after Daniel's desertion. She needed to break from of the "princess" reputation of being the youngest and the only girl in the family. Too sheltered by her big brothers.

Maybe that pampered, sheltered part of her had been why Daniel had left. If she'd seem stronger, would he have stayed?

At the back of the Miller house where the meeting as being held today, Kate stood swaying with her fussing *Bobbli*, the dark wings of her raven hair visible under her white *Kapp*. Seeing young Sarah pause by her mother to make faces at the *Bobbli* made Mercy smile.

After the sermons were over, Mercy went to join the women in Kate's kitchen. Her *Aenti* was of the older generation and it seemed fitting that Mercy, along with the other younger women, served lunch to the congregation.

"Hello!" she greeted Kate Miller cheerfully as she stepped from the crowd into the kitchen. "Would you like me to hold little Elizabeth? She seems fussy."

Kate heaved a sigh. "You don't mind?"

"No, of course not. I'm sure you need a break and the others probably can use your help getting the food out. Put me to work."

Gently shifting the *Boppli* to Mercy, Kate said, "Her colic started earlier today. I've never known it to be so bad. The poor little *Maedel*."

"Hey, I can dance and jiggle as well as you can." She glanced up, saying hesitantly, "You know, it might help her to have some Downy Wood Mint tea. It's helps with colic."

Already turning toward the kitchen, Kate paused. "Really? That would be wonderful!"

With a smile, Mercy said, "I'll brew some up for you to mix with water. She's so little, we have to make it milder."

"Bless you," said her friend, leaning forward to give her a squeezing hug before she hurried off.

"Welcome!" Kate beamed as she opened her door later that same day. "We're so glad you decided to come."

As was the custom, a youth Sing was being held at the same family home which had hosted the sermon.

"I didn't have much of a choice," Mercy admitted with a wry laugh as she shrugged out of her light coat. "*Onkle* and *Aenti* have almost bullied me into meeting unmarried *Menner*."

Kate laughed as she took Mercy's jacket. Without such a large crowd, the room was cooler now. "Well, no one will bully you here. We're just glad you came to enjoy the fun. Come in the kitchen. Sarah and the others are just helping me lay out the treats for later."

Smiling back, Mercy reflected that there was no way and no need to tell her hostess that *Onkle* and *Aenti* encouraged her to go to this Sing—even though it was hosted at Kate and Enoch's house—hoping Mercy would find any *Mann* who wasn't a Miller.

The house was already filling with a boisterous group of mostly younger people and she'd seen several volley ball nets set up in the yard outside. As at most Sings, a sprinkling of parents were also there as chaperons and to make sure the gathering didn't get too rowdy. Smiling at the young voices rising around her, Mercy followed Kate to the kitchen area. She saw Enoch standing to the side with young Sarah and another young man Mercy didn't recognize.

It annoyed her to notice that Isaac wasn't with them and, realizing this annoyed her even more. She brushed it aside with determination as she met the other women working with Kate.

Buggies could be heard rumbling up the drive outside and the noise in the house rose along with the temperature. Arranging baked goods on plates for later, Mercy worked alongside Kate's newly-found young cousin, Anna, and several others.

"We're so glad you could come," Anna said excitedly, scooping fresh-baked cookies off the hot tray young Sarah handed her and passing them over for Mercy to arrange on a plate for later. "We always have such good times. Of course, we'll sing later, but first we play games."

She made a face. "Some of the girls are really good at volley ball. I just try to hit the ball, but it's still great fun. What did you do at the Sings in your town?"

Mercy smiled. "Pretty much the same things, but the some of the boys would get carried away in playing volleyball and such."

"I know what you mean," Anna responded, looking wiser than her years. "Ours get crazy sometimes, doing stunts and diving after balls. It's silly."

"Attention! Attention!" Enoch stood on a chair, Isaac suddenly beside him, his blond hair gleaming.

"It's time to go out and pick teams for the games." Enoch was clearly trying to organize the group.

Mercy tried to ignore the sudden beating of her heart at the sight of Isaac. It was crazy to think anymore of one *Mann* than the other. She probably noticed him particularly because of *Onkle* and *Aenti's* silliness. What did it matter that Isaac grinned at her as if he'd been looking for her?

Following a stream of boisterous *youngies* out the door, Mercy still felt a little shy until several other girls about her age called her and Anna over. She'd met Miriam and Esther at the church service earlier—in between the *Menner* her *Onkle* kept bringing over—and it was natural for the four girls to fall into conversation.

"Here! Sit with us," Miriam invited, shifting to make room for them on a bench. "They'll be putting together the teams and then we can start."

"Let's just hope," Esther giggled, "we get put on a team with Aaron Yoder. Oh! He's your cousin, isn't he, Mercy?"

Scooping her skirt snug against her legs, Mercy happily sat next to Anna and the other girls. "Yes, and like a brother. Does he play well?"

"Yes! We all hope not to be on a team that plays against him." Esther peered around Miriam to say.

"He's rowdy!" Miriam scowled as she glared at the huddle of young men deciding the teams. "At one of our last Sings, my team played his and he was such a show-off that he spiked the ball right into my face!"

Esther laughed again. "Oh, you weren't hurt, Miriam. Just offended."

"I think I'd be offended, too." Mercy chuckled. "Did you manage to spill punch down his shirt later?"

"Mercy!" Despite her scandalized outcry, Esther gave another giggle.

"No, but when he had the nerve," Miriam snorted, "to ask to take me home in his buggy later, I said I'd made other arrangements."

"Aaron doesn't lack nerve," Mercy responded. "And he asked to drive you home later? Sounds like a boy. Are you sure he doesn't like you?"

Miriam sputtered. "Are you kidding? If that were true, I'd think he'd be nicer to me!"

"Yes," Mercy responded with an ironic chuckle. "Boys can be foolish."

"I'd just like a boy to ask to drive me home." Anna was wistful.

"Don't worry," Miriam responded, "several will eventually. And you think carefully before you say yes to any of them."

"Particularly if it's Isaac Miller." Esther giggled again.

"She's just saying that, Anna, because she's had her eye on him for a while, even though he's older." Miriam seemed to be the level-headed one. "Isaac's not as dangerous at volley ball as Aaron."

Mercy let their playful chatter roll over her, remembering the comradery of the girls she'd grown up with back home…before Daniel's desertion had turned their laughing jokes to scandalized whispers. They'd had such fun at the Sings, giggling like this and talking about who would take who home.

"*Shhh*," Esther admonished her friend. "Mercy will have some loyalty to her cousin. Don't talk about Aaron in front of her."

"Oh, go ahead," Mercy recommended to Miriam. "Don't mind me. I know him well enough to agree with most everything you said. Even if his *Mamm* and *Daed* think he walks on water, he's just a regular *Mann* like all the rest."

Across the yard, Enoch called out. "Okay. You know the rules. Let's start out with you counting around the circle, alternately calling out a number between one and four, that way we can pick four teams. I think we have enough for two games."

35

"I only hope I get on Isaac's team."

Mercy resisted the urge to roll her eyes at Esther's comment even as Miriam told her to hush. The girl was certainly out-going.

As they each called out a number, Mercy lost track of who was on which team, focusing on remembering her own.

"Okay," Enoch directed, "all the Ones over here. The Twos there and the Threes and Fours over there."

With lots of milling about the groups eventually gathered, several of the young men signaling their pleasure at being on teams together by clapping one another on the backs. Soon the four teams divided, with two going to the opposite sides of one net while the others stayed on the closest volleyball court outlined.

There was such a hubbub of chatter and laughter that Mercy felt her spirits lifting more than they had for weeks. When Enoch and his assistants had managed to herd the two teams to either court, the members spaced themselves out in preparation to play.

The boys had thrown off their coats to allow for more freedom of movement and Miriam called out in protest. "We have skirts! I think the boys should keep on their jackets to make the play fair."

"When is it ever fair between boys and girls?" called out a youth in laughter. "We *Menner* should get a little boost to help us out."

Still laughing at this byplay, Mercy didn't immediately notice who faced her across the net. Then she turned and saw fair-haired Isaac Miller smirking at her.

At least it looked like a smirk to her.

In his shirt sleeves with no jacket, his shoulders looked broad and his waist trim. She looked away, reminding herself that she shouldn't attend to Isaac Miller's physique, even if it did cause her heart to stutter a little.

This was not the measure of a *Mann. Gott* wished them to look at the inside.

Changing the direction of her thoughts with effort, she made a face at him in response to his smirky smile.

"Isaac, if you spike that ball into my face," she hissed in a lowered voice only he could hear, "I swear I'll find a way to slip valerian into your oatmeal somehow."

He laughed after giving the ball an assisting hit to send it several rows behind her. "What will valerian do to me?"

"Put you to sleep for a good long time," she promised, grimacing at him before she turned to join with her teammates in trying to hit the ball back. His laughter as she turned her back, rang in her ears.

When she turned back to face him, she saw that Isaac met her gaze.

"But Mercy, I have to help my team win!" He wiggled his eyebrows at her as he laughed again.

Before she could respond, the server at the back of the opposing court lofted the ball into the air again and the *youngie* next to her volleyed it back.

The play went back and forth then and other than her awareness of shouts rising from the other court, Mercy's attention was fully on the game between her team and Isaac's. It was soon clear, however, as the ball was sent back and forth across the net—with Isaac and several other guys on the team making many diving jumps to hit the ball before it touched the ground—that the teams weren't evenly matched.

Despite the shrieks of laughter and upraised voices from the other volley ball game, the one between her team and Isaac's demanded all her attention.

Rotating around to each take a turn at serving the ball, they gamely played on, despite the fact that the other team kept sending the ball back across the net, always where it bounced before being sent back.

"Mercy, hit it!" Esther shrieked from her position on the far side of Mercy's team.

Stretching to give the firm leather ball as strong a hit as she could, she felt again the warmth of belonging.

"That was a good hit," Isaac commented, saying in a teasing voice, "Anyone can see you are a strong young woman."

When she rolled her eyes, he lowered his voice again, "If only Abraham Swartz could see you. He'd know you could help in the fields and birth him a dozen more *Bopplies*."

Gasping at the cheekiness of his remark, Mercy reached up automatically to hit back the ball that flew in her direction.

Isaac continued teasing her. "I'm surprised your *Onkle* didn't mention this to him."

Several biting responses occurred to her, but none of them seemed either strong enough or appropriate, given the fact that the others around them would hear if she raised her voice. Instead of telling him he was a *Schaviut*—which he undoubtedly knew and would certainly be proud of—she just wrinkled her nose and made a face at him. He'd think it was a compliment to call him a rascal.

"Is your *Onkle* Yoder set on marrying you to a widow man?" Isaac teased in his lowered voice. "I believe there are several others for you to pick from."

Goaded, Mercy turned back to face him after having sent the ball back across the net. She retorted in a waspish undertone, "He isn't set on me marrying a widowed *Mann*, just anyone who isn't a Miller."

As soon as she said it, she felt her cheeks stain crimson and saw Isaac's grin broaden.

"Really? He said that? Well, since Enoch's married now and my two older brothers don't live close that just means me." Turning his back, he reached out strong arms clasped upward in an extended vee-shape and *thwacked* the ball over the net.

Isaac's team won the first game handily. It wasn't even close, but what the players on the losing team lacked in ability, Mercy recognized with disgust, they made up for in bravado. As soon as play ended for the first game, several of the *youngies* on Mercy's team cried out for a second match. The teams switched sides, the winners strolling to their new side while the vanquished challenging team went over to the opposite side, the undaunted *youngies* hooting and declaring their determination to win this game. The rest of the team followed dispiritedly.

As the game started, Mercy found herself on the back row, rotating toward the server position. Out of the corner of her eye, she saw her *Aenti* hovering near the edge of the court.

"Mercy!" the older woman called in a low voice.

Mercy leaned toward her, keeping one eye on the back and forth of the ball over the net.

"Was that Isaac Miller I saw you talking with? At the net?"

Running forward to bop the ball when it threatened to land in front of her, Mercy went back to her position. She really couldn't enter into a conversation right now. In low, repressive tone, she said, "Yes, *Aenti*. He's on the other team."

"Remember what your *Onkle* said about that family. I have two other *Menner* to introduce to you when you're finished playing."

Frustrated with the entire thing, Mercy turned aside from what she knew was a losing team effort. Responding to her *Aenti* with gritted teeth, her lips stretched into a smile in hopes of making her words more palatable, she said, "*Aenti*, you and *Onkle* must stop this. I'm not looking for a husband. I told you."

"And as we told you, Mercy, you must listen to those wiser. Your *Eldre* sent you to us—"

Just then the volley ball hit ground two feet from her and Mercy automatically swung round to see others on her team in a tangled heap from trying vainly to hit it back.

"Never mind, *Aenti*," she said, pushing back her spurting annoyance. "I can't talk now you see."

In the next few minutes she rotated through the server spot, relieved that her hit reclaimed some of her distracted mistake and at least went over the net. When her team shifted around again, Mercy went to the front row and looked across the net again into Isaac's teasing eyes.

"What's the matter, Mercy? Did your *Aenti* Yoder sidetrack you? I saw her there beside the court talking to you."

Determined not to miss another ball, Mercy lunged to the side just then to reach out and make an awkward return. Straightening to her place with the noise of the game all around them, she shot back at Isaac, "I just can't make *Onkle* and *Aenti* stop trying to marry me off to different *Menner*. She told me she has several more for me to meet after the game."

As soon as the words were out of her mouth, Mercy wished her temper hadn't prompted her to say anything to Isaac about this.

"Never mind. It's not your problem." she said hastily, stepping back to avoid the diving body of the *youngie* next to her who'd gotten seriously into the game.

"Maybe," he said with a laugh, "you should let one of the *Menner* court you. Just to get them off your back. You wouldn't have to actually marry him."

She stared at him as they shifted to the next rotation, struck by his teasing recommendation.

Maybe…she should do what he said. Or at least pretend to. A sudden pang of doubt shook her. She wouldn't want to be playing at this, though, if the *Mann's* heart was on the line. If she encouraged anyone to court her, it wasn't just her involved. She knew the distress a broken engagement could bring.

As she mulled over the thought, the volley ball flew over her head to fall just on the other side of the net and her team cheered.

Of course, she wouldn't have to be actually engaged, just courting, which was always done without telling the community. The trick was to find someone who wouldn't be serious about their courtship. Someone… Someone like Isaac. Who wasn't serious about much of anything, his niece aside.

The next day, Mercy and Hannah worked with Kate in her household garden, their skirts kilted up so they could squat down freely to press seed into the still-cool earth. A cool spring breeze drifted past every once in a while, even though they were into easing into early summer by that time.

"Tell me something," Mercy said after a few minutes of silence in their conversation. "Who is the old *Mann* with the sad face that I've seen at the services. I've passed him in the fields, too, and he just walks past, never seeming to see my wave."

After having seen him several times always looking the same, she felt a kinship, sensing some trouble sat on his soul.

"Old *Mann*?" Kate continued pressing seeds along her row.

"Yes. I've never seen a *Frau* with him or seen him talk to anyone at services. He's there, but not, if you know what I mean." Mercy scooted further along her row. "I wish my *Onkle* and *Aenti* would worry less about finding me a *Mann* and concentrate on matching others, if that's their bent. Maybe they could find a *Frau* for that unhappy old *Mann*."

"The one with gray hair and an angry face? Oh, Kate, she means Zacharius Graber," Hannah said from her corner of the garden.

"Oh! I was confused," Kate commented, "because I don't think of Zacharius Graber as sad. He does look somber and angry all the time. Of course, he has reason to be sad and angry. He doesn't need your *Onkle* to find him a *Frau* right now, though."

"*Yah*, he is grieving," Hannah agreed. "And angry, I suppose."

Mercy stopped her work for a moment, raising her face to the breeze before turning to ask, "Why?"

"Oh, his story is reason enough for his gloomy face." Kate shook her head. "He was single for many years and then he and *Frau* Graber seemed to see one other for the first time. They were both in middle years by then—she'd been married and widowed— and they really fell in love."

Hannah turned to start working her way down the next row. "It was remarkable. We were all so happy for them."

"That is fortunate," Mercy said from her garden row.

"*Yah*. They married and settled on his farm, which isn't far from Bishop Yoder's." Kate stood to slap some dirt off her hands. "There were no children, of course."

"And she had none from her first marriage, either." Hannah shook her head sadly. "*Gott's* ways are mysterious. She just never had a *Boppli*."

"Some women don't," Kate said in a practical voice. "I didn't conceive in my first marriage, either."

"*Neh*, but you and Jakob weren't married more than a few years," Hannah pointed out. "There's no knowing what might have happened if he hadn't died."

Silence fell over the garden plot as each woman continuing the planting and Mercy tried to imagine dour-faced Zacharius Graber being happy.

"But this Graber, where is his *Frau*? Did she leave him?" The thought left a sinking feeling in Mercy. She understood that only too well.

"*Neh*," Hannah stopped her planting long enough to look up sadly, "*Frau* Graber died suddenly. What? A year ago, Kate?"

"Something like that?" Her friend responded.

Just then Abigail and Lydia, Hannah's daughters, came pelting around the corner of the farmhouse with Sarah.

"*Mamm*! *Mamm*! There are little chickies in the hens' nests. Come see them!" Sarah was practically jumping up and down before she flopped down on the ground next to her mother.

"*Yah*, some just cracked through their eggshells, *Mamm*," Lydia said with the authority of an older child, "and you'd better tell the boys not to disturb the other eggs. The ones that have yet to open."

"Of course, not!" Hannah said sternly. "Tell your *Bruders* that I'll be very displeased if they disturb those eggs."

"I'll remind them!" Sarah said, jumping up gleefully.

"Is Elizabeth still asleep?" Kate halted her.

"Check her cradle before you go, please." She pointed to where it sat in a shady spot under a nearby tree.

"*Yah, Mamm*," Sarah tiptoed up to the cradle to report before she turned to run back to her mother with exaggerated stealth. "She's asleep still."

"*Gut*." Kate smacked a kiss on Sarah's cheek. "Now you can go make sure the boys leave the eggs alone."

When the girls had raced off, silence fell again over the garden until Kate broke it to say, "Zacharius Graber is still grieving…and does he seem more pale to you, Hannah?"

"Some. Some more pale," her friend replied, standing to go over to the rain barrel for a scoop of water. "*Yah*, that's *gut* water. Do you want some?"

"*Neh*," the other two women replied, still poking seeds into the moist earth.

"The old *Mann* seems so unhappy," Mercy finally said, even more troubled about him now that she knew he was a grieving widower.

"He does." Kate nodded. "He's been unhappy since Ada's death, but…do you remember, Hannah? He wasn't that way when we were children, back before he and Ada married."

"*Neh*." Hannah kept slowly dropping seeds. "He was a happy *Mann* back then, even though he had no *Frau*. Of course, we should remember that he's getting older now and our earthly bodies are frail."

Looking down at the small holes she pressed into the soil before dropping in seeds to be covered, Mercy said, "Sadness can make a body ill, more than age."

She looked up at her friends, not wanting to talk about herself, at this moment. "I think *Gott* would want us to…to reach out to this Zacharius Graber. Do you know if he has any friends?"

"We are all his friends, Mercy. But we don't know what to do to help him," Kate said. "*Frau* Bontreger told me that his heart is grieving within him. What do you do about a sad heart?"

"*Yah*." Hannah nodded. "He talks with no one—not even the bishops—and only every once in a while to old friends like the Bontregers and my husband's mother, Rachel."

"He looks so angry all the time." Kate wiped the back of her hand along her forehead.

"Maybe his sadness comes out that way," Mercy said. "I think I'll talk to him when I see him next."

Clearing her throat awkwardly two days later, Mercy stood at the open door of Isaac's woodshop. She'd taken the chance to stop by when on her walk back from Bontreger's store.

She'd mulled and mulled her situation over. She couldn't believe she was doing this and yet, what other choice did she have? Nothing she said to *Onkle* or *Aenti* Yoder seemed to sink in.

Inside a workshop that was attached to his barn, Isaac stood in his shirt sleeves before several braced planks of wood, a shaft of sunlight spilling over him and highlighting his fair hair and motes of shaved wood floating in the air.

"Mercy!" He called out, stopping in mid-sweep of his wood plane. "Come in. What are you doing here? I'm surprised your *Onkle* and *Aenti* have let you come see me." He flashed a teasing smile her way as she stepped into the woodshop that had boards of different sizes leaning haphazardly against the walls.

Taking a deep breath in hopes of quieting her thundering heart, she swallowed hard and said, "That's why I've come."

He laughed. "Don't tell me, they sent you."

Pushing a smoothing hand across the plank, Isaac swept wood dust to the powdery floor as he waited for her response.

"No." She stopped in front of his work bench. "No, *Onkle* and *Aenti* don't know I'm here."

The gaze he sent her was filled with arrested interest. "Really? Tell me more."

While Isaac had certainly enjoyed his sparring conversations with the pretty Amish princess, he'd not gotten the impression she was bowled over by his charms. She certainly wasn't here because she found him so fascinating.

Standing in front of his work bench, a black *Kapp* over her flaxen head and the skirt of her dark green dress falling to just above the floor that was covered in wood dust, Mercy didn't immediately respond. Isaac found himself completely disregarding the plank in front of him. This was getting more and more interesting.

"Come sit." Isaac dusted his hands together before picking up a rag to pass over the cowhide seat of a chair to the side, dusting it clean. "Have a seat."

She seemed undecided about the chair and since he was concerned she'd turn and leave, he pulled a stool for himself over close to the chair and perched on it to encourage her to sit down, as well. "Tell me. Why have you come?"

"Isaac…" Mercy finally sat down, taking another deep breath. She looked at him with a considering gaze before saying abruptly, "you seem…up for anything. I mean, you tease and joke around. You tease more than most."

"I do," he admitted, a little rueful.

With a smile that seemed tense, she went on, "Do you remember what you said to me the other night when we were playing volley ball before the singing?"

Laughing, he shrugged. "You know, I say a lot of things. Which do you mean?"

"Isaac," she said, seeming to grow more decided as determination settled onto her face, "remember you suggested I find someone to pretend to court me? To get *Onkle* and *Aenti* to stop throwing other *Menner* at me?"

"Yes," he said slowly. It had been a joking suggestion off the top of his head when he saw her plight, but Isaac hadn't really thought about it. "You mean you are considering this? Truly?"

Seeming to suddenly see where dust from the chair had marked her skirt, she brushed at it and then said, "Yes."

"Oh, my." He felt a little stunned. He was so used to his friends and family laughing at his silly, hare-brained antics that he wasn't accustomed to being taken seriously. Getting a laugh was usually the point. Isaac certainly hadn't intended that Mercy should take this suggestion to heart.

She hurried into speech again. "Isaac, I've tried and tried to get them to understand. To give me a moment to catch my breath and not to try to rush me in marriage with pretty much anyone."

"Except me," he stuck in with a grin, unable to stop himself.

"Yes. Except you. That's part of why you seem…perfect for this." She managed to look both self-conscious and determined. "That and because I wouldn't be deceiving you in this pretend courtship."

"Ooookay." He studied her for a moment, seeing a strong sense of purpose on her face.

She said after a moment, "Try to understand, Isaac. I know the…difficulties…of being jilted by someone. I don't want to visit that on anyone else. Anyone who thought it was real. The courtship, I mean."

He felt the pain in her voice like a shard of ice through his heart. He'd done that to her, encouraged Daniel to run off to the *Englisch* world. Not that he'd meant it or ever thought the *Mann* would actually jilt Mercy and leave his life here.

"Of course." Isaac shifted on his stool, hating the guilt that ate at him. "You wouldn't want that. To have a *Mann* think you meant to marry him and then pine for you."

"No."

She was so pretty with her fair skin and blue eyes, sitting there in his shop like a morsel. It flashed over Isaac how sweet it would be to have a loving wife come out to his shop and sit like that as he crafted beds and chests and cradles.

How could Daniel have left her? How could Isaac have thoughtlessly challenged Daniel to do something that would lead to him hurting her?

"So, I'm asking you, Isaac. Will you do it?" Mercy looked at him with a level blue gaze. "Will you pretend to court me so *Onkle* and *Aenti* will stop trying to get me married off?"

He stared at her a moment.

"You know I am the last *Mann* they want to you court, right?" he asked. "You said as much yourself."

Mercy flushed a little, looking mulish. "Yes, I know…and I don't care. Maybe that's another reason why you're so perfect for this."

He said slowly, "You want to punish them a little."

"Maybe," she sounded defensive, brushing her hand again against her skirt. "It's not like we're going to really get married. This is pretend. It's a courtship to give me a break from their constant matchmaking."

Another grin spread across his face, "So, we're just going to court and spend time together and talk…at your *Onkle's* house? Go for buggy rides? I can see him squirming."

"Yes." Her gaze was steady. "Squirming won't hurt him."

"No, it won't." Isaac knew he probably shouldn't agree to this, certainly Enoch and their brothers, James and Elijah would tell him not to do it. Well, Elijah might see the fun in it.

And, although no one else knew of his having angrily teased Daniel about being unable to make it in the *Englischer* world, Isaac felt he owed it to Mercy to help her. After all, she wouldn't be in this situation if it weren't for him.

"Okay." The word came out of him decisively. "Okay, Mercy Yoder. I'm in. Let's pretend to court. Starting now…can I drive you home in my buggy?"

CHAPTER FOUR

Despite the weather warming from spring into summer, the air cooled as the sun sank. Mercy shivered a little in her seat on the carriage box next to Isaac as they sat behind the *clip-clopping* horse as he drove her home that afternoon.

"Here." He dropped the reins to shrug out of his coat.

"That's okay," she said hastily, very conscious that she'd gotten him into the situation, her cheeks burning at the remembrance that she'd actually asked him to do this. Isaac was only pretending to court her. She didn't think that qualified her to demand his jacket from him.

With the reins dropped, the horse came to a standstill as Isaac took off his coat. "Don't be silly."

He draped it around her shoulders and his evocative male scent surrounded her. If she hadn't been so annoyed with *Onkle* and *Aenti's* craziness, she would never have had the nerve to ask such a pretense of Isaac.

He picked up the reins again and clucked for the horse to move. It obediently set forward and she mentally noted that the horse seemed to trust him. She'd seen *Menner* take out their anger on their horses, but Isaac's seemed to have no fear of him. Even Daniel had seemed impatient with his nag.

The thought streaked through her mind and she wondered who cared for Daffodil now that Daniel was gone.

With the day light fading, they drove in the late afternoon dimness only occasionally darkened by a passing cloud. It hit

Mercy how right this felt, despite the fact that everything between her and Isaac was pretense.

"So," he said in a matter-of-fact voice, "tell me about your home."

Just the thought of her snug home with *Mamm* and *Daed* and her brothers nearby sent a pang through Mercy. She missed them all so much. Remembering the wet snuffles of their big dog, Jasper, made her eyes suddenly damp.

Clearing her throat, she began talking of home. "...and Levi and Micah live nearby and have just bought farms of their own. Only Joseph is now married. I expect the others will marry soon, though. Ethan's courted several girls, but seems in no hurry to take a *Frau*..."

Isaac turned his head to say, "You have five older brothers, don't you?"

"Yes. Levi, Caleb, Micah, Joseph and Elijah." When her *Eldre* had thought she needed to get away from Elizabethtown after Daniel ditched her, her oldest brother, Levi had been against it. He said she'd done nothing wrong and had no need to hide.

But her parents had felt strongly that a summer spent with *Onkle* and *Aenti* Yoder in Mannheim would be good for her. If only she'd known how determined her relatives would be to marry her off.

"And you the youngest, the only girl." Isaac spoke in a teasing voice.

"*Yah*." Her confirmation came out on a dry note. She knew what was said of her.

"You princess, you. All those older brothers to fetch and run for you." He said it in such a funning tone that she couldn't really take offense.

Mercy glanced over at him. "And tease me and leave me trailing after them and always out-do me."

"What? They didn't shelter and pamper you? And do all the chores?"

"*Neh*. I had chores." She reflected on the matter. "I suppose they did shelter me—aren't brothers supposed to do that?—but pamper me? No. What farm child is pampered? There are always chickens to feed and weeds to pull in the garden."

"When did you have time to learn about herbs?"

It startled her that Isaac knew this about her and she looked over quickly.

"Kate told me," he said.

Mercy knew he must have seen—even in the late afternoon light—the questioning look she threw him. "Oh. Kate. Yes, I've talked with her about it some. I may have a remedy that will ease little Elizabeth's crying."

"That will be a relief for all." Isaac said in a sincere voice as they turned on to the road that led to her *Onkle's Haus*. "Enoch walks the floor with the *Boppli* every night."

"I know. Poor everyone. It's so hard when a *Boppli* struggles."

"And Kate's very good at being a *Mamm*. She raised Sarah after the *Maedel's Mamm* died—you know Sarah's the child of Kate's first husband?"

"*Neh*, I did not realize she's not Enoch's blood *Dochder*. They seem so...."

Isaac smiled. "I know. Kate married Enoch a year or so after her husband died. She and Sarah had been living with her *Eldre* after Jakob's death and then her *Eldre* both died a year later in a buggy accident. It was terrible."

"I can imagine. I'm glad she and Enoch found one another...and he's such a wonderful *Daed* to both girls—Sarah and the *Boppli*."

Isaac clucked to turn his horse into the Yoder drive and Mercy puzzled over how she could feel both relief and regret that their ride was over.

"Yes, he is a good *Daed*. How did you learn about herbal treatments?" After reining the buggy to a stop in front of the Yoder house, Isaac leaned an elbow on his knee, seeming in no rush to leave.

Mercy swallowed as she thought about eventually presenting Isaac to her *Onkle* and *Aenti* as a suitor. They'd pull solemn, worried faces and ask her if she'd not heard them. It served them right, since neither had listened to her pleas.

"My *Grossmammi* taught me." Just the thought of the old woman brought a smile to Mercy's mouth. "She lived with us and let me follow her into the fields when I was a little *Maedel*—as long as I'd done my chores. *Grossmammi* knew so much about natural treatments."

"It seems she passed on much of her skill to you." He tilted his head back and she saw the strong line of his throat in the moonlight that shone on them.

Mercy told herself sternly that she shouldn't have this physical flush in reaction to Isaac. He was doing her a favor in pretending to court her because she'd asked for his help and his joking nature led him to respond. *Onkle* Yoder hadn't endeared himself to the Miller boys, it seemed.

"I don't think I'll ever have all *Grossmammi's* knowledge, but I'll be glad if I can help Kate and Enoch and *Boppli* Elizabeth."

Isaac nodded toward the house. "Shall I come in?"

"Not now, I think," Mercy said with decision. "*Aenti* are probably getting the meal on the table. I'll tell them tomorrow that you brought me home. They expected I'd walk home as that's how I started out."

"Whatever you say." He got down from the buggy and reached a steadying hand to her as she descended to the gravel drive. "Are you sure you want to tell them by yourself?"

He shook his head. "They really don't like us Millers."

Mercy chuckled at the fake puzzlement in his voice as she removed his coat from her shoulders and handed it back. "I'm sure I'll be fine."

"Good," Isaac said, taking her chilled hand and wrapping it around his arm, firm beneath the cotton of his white shirt sleeve. He slung his coat over his opposite shoulder, saying as he walked her to the door. "When shall I come to sit with you? We could take a walk and you can show me some herbs in the wild."

"As if you care," she retorted. "I wouldn't bore you with that."

"I won't be bored." His tone was surprised as they mounted the steps to the porch, as if she ought to expect him to simply enjoy her company.

Mercy felt herself flush in the darkness.

"I tell you what." She considered him, the faint light from the rising moon now blocked by the porch roof. "Come over this Sunday afternoon. We have no service this week and I will have had time to break the news to *Onkle* and *Aenti* that they don't need to keep trying to match me with someone."

"Because you've found a match on your own." He completed the thought with a chuckle. "Such as it is."

It hit her again how much Isaac was helping her and she said with a sudden clutch at his arm, "Thank you, Isaac. I know this is a lot to ask. I just want you to know how much I appreciate your willingness to do it."

In the dim light, a smile twisted his lips. "No sacrifice, Mercy. I'm very willing to pretend to court you."

"Sarah, *Leibling*, move the plane this way over the wood." His hands over her small ones, Isaac guided her in the motions several days after his startling conversation with Mercy in the same wood shop. And their drive home.

He'd enjoyed her company...maybe too much as he felt responsible for her plight.

Chuckling, Enoch shifted back on the stool beside Isaac's work bench. "I don't know why you're bothering, *Bruder*. It's not like Sarah's going to follow in your steps and build her own furniture. She'll have a husband who can do that and you need to tend your farm."

Samuel, sitting nearby in the very leather chair Isaac had dusted for Mercy when she'd visited him here, looked on as sunlight pooled at his feet. "Isaac's spending less time on his furniture and more on the crops. And Sarah will have her choice of suitors, won't you?"

"I don't know, *Grossdaddi*," she said with a cheeky grin, her hand still moving with Isaac's. "I hope I have suitors."

"Well, this way, she'll be able to teach her *Mann* a thing or two." Isaac ignored his brother's jibe about the farm. He knew the family concern that he spent too much time here in the woodshop and his efforts would be better given to his farming. "Here, Sarah, run your hand over the wood to see how smooth it is."

"Because that's what draws *Menner*," Enoch said sardonically. "A *Maedel* who can teach them something."

Their father laughed at this.

"It's not like you married a mouse. Sarah's been raised by a mother who knows her own mind." Isaac turned around to reach for sand paper to smooth the planed board on his work bench. Mousey women had never drawn him, for sure. Was that why Daniel had left Mercy? He wanted a more subservient *Frau*? Of course, that hadn't made him leave the church. Isaac knew very well the part he'd played in Daniel doing that.

"This is very true." Enoch agreed, getting to his feet. "Come on, Sarah. It's time to get back to the *Haus*. You can work with your *Onkle* Isaac another time. You'll find him out here often enough."

"Okay." Sarah dusted her hands together as Isaac had shown her before hugging him. "Goodbye, *Onkle*. Goodbye, *Grossdaddi*."

"Goodbye, *Liebling*." Watching as she went to hug Samuel, Isaac rustled through the sand paper for the right grit to further smooth the board for the small bed he was making for *Boppli* Elizabeth.

It had occurred to him to mention Mercy's request to Enoch and Samuel, but Isaac had stopped. This seemed private between him and Mercy, although he didn't doubt that his *Bruder* would appreciate the grief his courting Mercy would give Bishop Yoder.

Still, this was the kind of thing his *Daed*—as well as, Enoch, James and Gideon—would recommend he not do, calling him a *Schaviut*. But even though his rascal urges might have drawn him to the pretense, that wasn't why he'd agreed.

He felt he owed Mercy.

"That's quite a sturdy bed you're building that *Boppli*. Mayhap Enoch's right, though, and your time would be better spent on your fields."

"My fields are just fine and the *Boppli's* Enoch's *Dochder*," was Isaac's wry response. "I figure she'll have quite a kick to her. The bed needs to be sturdy."

"Probably so. Your *Mamm* used to say the same about Enoch," his father commented, nodding.

Isaac didn't want to think about what his *Mamm*—or Samuel—would say about his thoughtless remarks to Daniel several years ago. He hadn't even been a foolish *youngie* then, but a *Mann* fully grown. He cringed just remembering how he'd teased the other *Mann* that the *Englischer* world was too tough for him. That Daniel could never make it without his sheltering family.

It would have been easier to forgive himself if he hadn't been so angry with Daniel's boasting at the time. Nothing good was done out of anger.

The older and wiser had warned Isaac over and over that his teasing and joking would one day have a bad fallout and it had certainly had results he'd never intended.

"I should be going, too," Samuel said, not getting out of his chair. "This is a perfect time for tilling the field, now that winter has finally given way to warmer weather. I know you're watching your fields for tilling time."

"I think I'm going to court Mercy Yoder." The abrupt words were out of Isaac's mouth before he realized it.

His father considered him a moment.

"Well, are you?" Samuel said, still without a lot of reaction. "She's a comely enough girl. More than most."

"Yes. I like her." Isaac realized as he said the words that it was true. He did like Mercy. His heart warmed as he remembered her kind offer of help with Sarah that day in Bontreger's store and the way she'd talked about learning herbal remedies from her *Grossmammi*. "She's not a…princess, like some say."

"*Neh?*"

"No." Isaac ran the rough paper over the plank again. "She's different than I expected. Nicer. Definitely pleasing to the eye."

He looked up to meet his father's gaze. "Maybe even worth spending time at the Yoder's *Haus* to court her."

"Well," his *Daed* said as he finally got to his feet. "You've certain flitted around enough flowers to know a good one when you see it. I hope all goes well. See you later, *der Suh*."

"Goodbye, *Daed*."

Isaac drew a deep breath, pausing in his sanding. He'd prayed to *Gott* for forgiveness so often after learning of Daniel's choice. He knew *Gott* forgave him. He just struggled to do it himself.

Maybe this would help. Maybe being a service to Mercy in this way would atone a little for his sin.

Two days later, Bishop Yoder stood holding his front door opened. "Isaac Miller, what do you mean you're here to see Mercy?"

The old *Mann's* white beard seemed to bristle with indignation.

Hiding his grinning response, Isaac said, "Um, well, Bishop, I like her and…I'd like to visit with her. Did she not tell you I would come today? We decided I would when I drove her home."

Bishop Yoder didn't respond for a moment, just standing in the opening as if to bar Isaac's entrance.

"*Yah*. I heard you drove her home went she'd walked to Bonteger's store." There was both disapproval and suspicion in his voice.

"Um, can I come in?" Isaac nodded at the doorway, his hat in his hand.

"*Yah*, I suppose so," Bishop Yoder said, stepping back reluctantly.

Maintaining a pleasant face—which he knew would annoy the older *Mann* even more—Isaac moved past him into the house. Services had often been held here, so he knew the home, but he also knew better than to assume anything, so he stood waiting to be asked to sit down on the stark wooden settle in front of the fire.

"Sit!" Bishop Yoder finally barked, nodding toward the settle.

Just then Isaac heard steps on the stairs as Mercy came into the room, a smile on her fair face.

In her small black *Kapp* and dark green dress, she was beautiful and he wished her glowing smile was for more than her *Onkle's* benefit.

"Isaac!"

Her hand was outstretched to him and he took it with a buzzing sense of unreality, aware of how small her hand felt in his. It wasn't the first time. He'd taken her hand to help her into and out of his buggy…wrapped her hand around his arm as he walked her up the steps here when he'd driven her home after her shocking request. Still, his heart kicked into gallop mode now and he found himself grinning back like a fool.

How could Daniel have left her? They were bade to mind the inner heart, but her exterior seemed pretty nice, too. Had Daniel asked Mercy to join him in an *Englisch* life?

"Come sit, Isaac," she invited. "Let me take your hat. Would you like some lemonade? I put just a sprig of mint and some blueberries in it. Very good! You'll see."

This last was added, he knew, after surprise dawned on his face as he lowered himself to the settle.

"That sounds…sounds very *gut*."

Her smile widened. "You'll like it. I promise."

"Is that your *Grossmammi* Yoder's recipe?" Bishop Yoder stopped in mid-exit from the living room, staring at Mercy with the same outraged look on his face, as if he had something against lemonade with mint and blueberries.

"*Neh, Onkle*." Mercy wore an innocent expression. "My *Grossmammi* Schwartz."

"*Hmph*," her *Onkle* responded. Having made this contribution to the conversation, he left the room in the direction of the kitchen.

"It is good!" Isaac took another drink.

Mercy rolled her eyes as she sat on the chair opposite him. "Well, don't sound so surprised."

Still chewing a berry as the door her *Onkle* had gone through opened again, Isaac said, "I've just never thought of blueberries in drinks."

Frau Yoder came into the room sedately carrying a basket from which spilled what looked like a work shirt. She nodded as she lowered herself onto another chair. "Good afternoon, Isaac Miller."

"I hope you are well, *Frau* Yoder."

"As well as can be expected," responded the elderly woman, launching into a recital of her aches and pains as she pulled the unfinished work shirt from her sewing basket.

When she paused, Mercy jumped in to say, "Let us play a card game, Isaac."

"Certainly." He couldn't help smiling at her, before adding in a teasing voice. "Let's hope you're better at cards than you are at volley ball."

Going to get the cards from a drawer, she scoffed. "Brave words, brave words. We'll see."

An hour later, Isaac sat back as Mercy laid a winning hand on the table in front of him. "Again? What is this evil gift of yours?"

"Skill!" she chortled in response. "You're just not that *gut* at cards!

Mercy's *Aenti* Yoder—who had been in and out of the room several times as they played—made a clucking noise of faint disapproval as Mercy succumbed again to chuckles of merriment.

"Mercy!" Martha Yoder admonished as she sank back into her chair, not seeming surprised that her niece made no response to her.

"I tell you what," With a glance at her disapproving *Aenti*, Isaac placed a hand over Mercy's to interrupt her card shuffling. "Let's go for a walk. You can show me where the best herbs and wildflowers grow."

Hoping Isaac hadn't noticed her quickly indrawn breath at his touch— Mercy reminded herself she had to stop doing that every time his hand brushed hers—she said as calmly as she could, "Of course…because you never know when you might need a Bee Balm tea or a chest poultice of some kind."

"Mercy!" her *Aenti* repeated in a scandalized voice, as if referring to the male chest was shocking.

"*Neh*, you never do know," Isaac retorted. "Come show me."

"Okay," she rose to her feet to put the cards in their drawer before following him to the door. Mercy glanced back at Martha Yoder. "I'll be here in time to help with supper, *Aenti*."

"*Yah*, *Nibling*." The older woman looked doubtful, but made no other comment.

As the front door closed behind them, Isaac exhaled as he descended the steps, "Ahhh! Well, that was interesting."

"Very," she agreed. "Maybe now they'll stop scouring around for *Menner* to introduce me to."

"Are you kidding?" Isaac looked over his shoulder as she descended to stand beside him. "I wouldn't be surprised if your *Onkle* stepped it up. Just to tempt you away from me."

She chuckled again. He had a point. When Isaac came to see her, *Onkle* had looked so flustered he couldn't speak.

"Here." Isaac took her hand as they started down the drive, commenting, "They may be looking."

Doing her best to ignore the heart flutter that came with his touch, Mercy said calmly, "So which way do you want to walk?"

He glanced at her with surprise. "Whichever way the best herbs grow."

"Really?" She shouldn't have loved the strong feel of his hand around hers—which he maintained even when they'd walked a ways from the house—but she did. It's-just-for-pretend, she chanted to herself.

"Of course. Where do you go on your herb-gathering walks?"

"We can turn this way." She took her hand from his to hold back a gate that led onto a fallow field next to the drive.

"Okay."

They ambled along together over the weedy, grown-up ground in silence for a while and Mercy felt the usual peace of the surroundings begin to filter into her.

"I love this," she said after a few moments. "Walking through the fields like this. I used to do it with my *Grossmammi* Schwartz, from when I started to walk."

"That's a while back," Isaac commented.

She felt his tentative gaze on hers before he said, "Did...Daniel go on herb-gathering walks with you?"

Mercy looked over sharply. "How did...? What do you know of Daniel?"

They kept walking, reaching another fence before he answered.

Isaac held back a long, thorny branch for her. "You spoke of having been jilted... I know you were to marry Daniel Stoltzfus."

Mercy held back a wince at the word, even though she'd used it herself. It was accurate, though. Daniel had jilted her.

Walking across another field toward a thin vein of stream, shadowed over by trees, she said nothing.

After a few minutes, Isaac said in a voice that seemed carefully casual, "I met him, you know."

"Daniel?" She looked over quickly. "How could you know Daniel?"

"I didn't really know him. I just met him, I said. He was here—maybe a year or a year and a half back—visiting relatives of his." He swished through the long grass with a stick he'd picked up.

"Then you know all about it." The words felt brittle as they came out of her. She was surprised that he'd agreed to pretending courtship...if he knew her former fiancé.

"Probably not," Isaac responded after they walked on toward the stream. "Just the gossip, really. I've heard that Daniel left you—and the church for the *Englisch* world—right before you two were published to marry."

Mercy said nothing, brooding over her tainted situation. Finally, she said in a hard voice, "Two weeks before we were to marry. I came here to Mannheim to move beyond the whispers. That's why *Onkle* and *Aenti* are so determined to marry me off. It's almost as if they think I need to prove by getting some other *Mann* to marry me that I didn't cause Daniel to leave."

Isaac stopped suddenly, his grasp on her arm pulling her to a stop, as well. "That's ridiculous! You are not to be blamed for his actions."

The intensity of his reaction startled her. Mercy could only stare.

"How could you have caused him to act in that manner? It is silly." With his hand still on her arm, he scowled fiercely at her.

"N-no. I could not." She looked up at him, stupidly aware again of his touch, struck again by the vividness of his blue gaze.

"And it's not as if you left our life. You have not run off to the *Englisch*, as well, but you didn't." Isaac's hand finally fell.

"No, but it doesn't matter, Isaac." She felt almost kind as she explained the awkwardness of her situation. "It's an association. How many *Eldre* fear that their sons and daughters will leave the church and be drawn into the sinful *Englisch* life?"

As they started again crossing toward the stream, now burbling more loudly as they grew closer, Mercy reached to pat his shoulder. "It's only natural that I should be considered…nervously. They do not know why he left. They have to wonder if I had anything to do with it. Even I do not know why he left."

"If you had anything to do with Daniel's actions, you would have left with him," Isaac snapped. "It's *narrish*—just crazy—to consider it your fault. No one should blame you."

Mercy drew in a breath, a tremulous smile growing on her face. "Come see what grows here next to the stream."

Although this courtship was all a pretense, she suddenly felt less alone now.

The next day, Mercy stood next to her friend at the roadside farm stand. "I'm so glad Kate suggested I help you sell your vegetables, Hannah."

"*Yah*, we've had a bumper crop this year and I like to bring in some extra money when possible." Frizzy blonde curls escaped Hannah's bun, springing out from beneath her white *Kapp*.

"I'm glad to assist," Mercy arranged the deep purple eggplants. "It's nice to be outdoors."

The farm stand extended over several stalls, with a graveled drive allowing customers to pull over to make purchases. Having arrived only several minutes ago in Hannah's buggy, Mercy had noticed Isaac at the far stall almost immediately. She could see several graceful chairs that had been set in front of that part of the roadside stand and guessed he was helping a neighbor unload and set up. *Englischers* often liked to buy sturdy Amish furniture.

Their time together the day before when he visited her at her *Onkle's* had been very nice and although he'd only done it as a favor, she liked to think that after their walk, they were becoming friends.

Several *Englischers* had already parked their cars in front of the stand and were now browsing amongst the baskets of broccoli and dark-red beets. The mounds of vegetables made splashes of bright color: lettuce and pale green and purple cabbages next to bunches of jaunty orange carrots which were adjacent to the white cauliflower and deep purple eggplant. There was a lovely scent to freshly-picked vegetables mixed with a faint leftover tang of manure fertilizer.

Settling back in one of the folding chairs Sarah had brought, Mercy asked, "Do you sell here every summer?"

Hannah nodded vigorously. "*Yah*, and most falls, too, when the pumpkins are in. I enjoy growing things and so I make a big garden every year. Did you not notice the patch on the side of the house?"

"I did indeed. My *Mamm* always has a lovely garden and she made a special part to the side for my *Grossmammi* Schwartz to put in a few herbs we couldn't get as freely from the fields around the house."

Just talking about her family left Mercy's chest feeling tight.

"That's right!" Hannah perked up. "Kate said you gather medicinal herbs. Whatever you gave her seems to have helped *Bobbli* Elizabeth's crying fits."

"I'm so glad." Mercy smiled. "*Grossmammi* would make it for the *Mamms* around us when I was a *Maedel*."

She glanced down the short row of stalls. "You have a nice stand here. The one at home isn't quite as long. I help my *Aenti* Schwartz at the stand there in Elizabethtown from time to time. Did I see a furniture stall at the other end?"

"Oh, *yah*. You should go see all the things Isaac Miller makes to sell. He's quite a wonder with wood." Hannah nodded.

"Isaac?" Mercy stared at her. "He's an actual woodcrafter? He does more than repairs? I mean, I knew he has a workshop, but I never would have suspected he does it seriously."

She thought for a moment. "I wouldn't think Isaac did much of anything seriously."

The other woman laughed.

"*Yah*. He builds beds and tables, chairs. Most everything. Abel Glick taught Isaac everything he knew." Hannah repinned her shifted *Kapp*. "As a boy, Isaac was always in Abel's workshop. Abel built everything. He had quite a gift from *Gott*. It was such a good joke that everyone called Isaac old Abel's shadow. Of course, Abel's gone now, but Isaac learned very well how to turn a table leg and a bedpost. With Abel no longer here, Isaac builds whatever is needed hereabouts and makes a good amount from the *Englischers* that stop by. I've heard Enoch and the other brothers, James and Gideon, teasing Isaac about spending too much time making furniture. But I've never thought he ignores his farm to do it. You should go see his offerings."

The thought of frisky, *narrish* Isaac Miller doing something as grounded and painstaking as building beautiful, plain furniture— all the while maintaining a farm—was surprising. Mercy glanced over at Hannah. "I thought he just had the farm. I mean from what *Onkle* said."

"Oh, he does have one." Having gotten up to settle an early tomato that was teetering on the edge of a basket, Hannah spoke over her shoulder. "All the Miller boys have farms. Their *Mamm* and *Daed* made sure to save the money for it. I believe they even helped their *Dochders* and their *Menner* get farms. Isaac is the youngest of seven, I think. His two older sisters live in other towns, too. Like the other two brothers. But he alone has this way with wood."

"Only Enoch, Isaac and—what's their younger sister's name? Lizzie?—live here?" Out of the corner of her eye, Mercy spotted Isaac to the far side, laughing with the elderly woman who displayed baked goods in the stall next to them.

"It must keep him busy, making furniture and running his farm." She was still trying to get her head around this new picture of the *Mann* who was *verrickt* enough to enter into the pretense she'd suggested.

After a lull in customers, Hannah urged. "Go look at *Frau* Troyer's cakes and bread and Isaac's rocking horses. I'm thinking of getting him to make us a new cradle. My little James was probably the last *Boppli* that should sleep in the old one."

"Are you sure I shouldn't stay with you?" Mercy asked. "I'm here to help, you know."

Hannah laughed, waving a hand toward the empty booth. "As you can see, we aren't overrun with customers now."

"*Neh*," she laughed in response, brushing a hand against her gray skirt as she got up. "Okay. I'll take a quick look around."

Walking around the booth to the customer side, Mercy strolled past the bread, cakes and pies in Frau Troyer's booth. The smells were tantalizing and several *Englischers* stood trying to decide between them.

"Hey there, Mercy Yoder!" Isaac called out as a couple left his booth carrying two chairs with them to their big shiny car.

"Hello, Isaac," she responded, walking toward his end of the farm stand. "I see you've made a sale. I would never have taken you for a furniture builder."

"And why not?"

His wicked grin tugged at her, making her want to smile back. "You're like a butterfly, Isaac. Here and there and all over. I've just never realized you can stay in one place long enough to...to build a chair."

"Ah, but there's a lot you don't know about me yet." He shifted one of the many chairs around the booth, motioning her to sit. "See? It's even comfortable. I'm not the good-for-nothing you think."

Sighing exaggeratedly as if she were humoring him, Mercy went over to sit in the chair.

Just as she lowered herself, she saw Zacharius Graber walking morosely down the road towards the farm stand. To her surprise, he turned in and walked past she and Isaac, heading for *Frau* Troyer's baked goods booth.

"Good afternoon, Mr. Graber," she called as he passed, as usual feeling drawn to him. Mercy didn't know why, but his sadness tugged at her.

The old man glanced over.

She nodded her *Kapped* head to him. "I'm Mercy Yoder. I hope your day is *gut*."

Zacharius Graber's steps slowed and he looked over at her, glowering. "As *gut* as any other, *Maedel* Yoder."

With those brief, gruff words, he continued walking toward the other booth.

"Do not let him upset you," Isaac commented, having situated himself in a chair next to her. "Old man Graber is irritable to everyone."

"He just seems so sad." Mercy watched him stand in front of the bread.

"I suppose he is," Isaac returned, reaching out to take her hand in his. "Although he looks angry mostly."

64

Mercy swung back to look into Isaac's face, aware that his touch was having its usual effect on her flesh. She drew in a deep breath, saying in a quiet tone. "What's this? Are you afraid I'll grab a chair and run away with it?"

He lifted her hand and smiled into her face. "There are others around. We are courting now. Remember? I think you'd allow me to take your hand if that were so."

In a sudden realization, she recognized that when Daniel had held her hand in times past, she'd never felt this streak of lightening through her body. Just as soon as the awareness fluttered through her, she felt a pang of guilt. Shouldn't she have felt that same sizzle with the *Mann* she was to marry? Certainly more than with Isaac, who was no more to her than a friend.

"You do a good business here? Selling furniture?" She forced the casual words through a throat that suddenly felt too tight.

"Yes."

He kept smiling at her and she felt concerned that the flush beneath her skin was growing too pink not to be noticed.

"We get a good traffic of *Englischers* and other folk," he said. "Hey, you should see if you can sell your herbs here, too. Others have colicky *Bopplies*. Kate and Enoch have talked of the benefit your mixture gave Elizabeth. Don't you also make salves and solutions that give many different aids?"

"*Yah.* Yes, I do. You think others would buy them?"

"Of course. Why not use *Gott's* gifts rather than go to *Englischer* doctors? And just think," Isaac grinned at her again. "We can work here together."

CHAPTER FIVE

"Sarah! Over here!" Mercy called several days later, pointing to a bright yellow butterfly that had landed on a stalk nearby and rested, opening and closing its wings every now and then.

The girl crossed *Aenti* Yoder's garden and came to stand at Mercy's side. "Oh, it's so beautiful!"

Almost as if responding to all the attention, the butterfly suddenly soundlessly floated off to a farther stalk.

Laughing, Mercy stood with Sarah, watching it delicately land and balance on a plant that moved gently with the light breeze that was filled with warming, earthy scent of spring.

"Have we planted all the herbs yet?" The *Maedel* bent to gently touch one green tip.

"All these. We still have the others."

Kate came around the side of the Yoder farm house, carrying *Boppli* Elizabeth. "All changed, dry and happy."

She jiggled her daughter, holding her up to catch the breeze and sun. "It's so nice to be in the warm sun, isn't it, *Liebling*?"

They all laughed as the *Boppli* gurgled, reaching for a puffy cloud.

"Okay, let's put Elizabeth in her chair right next to the garden and we'll get back to work."

Poking a hole in the damp, cool soil with her finger, Mercy carefully dropped in a seedling. "I really appreciate the two of you helping me with the planting."

"Of course!" Kate sent her a twinkling smile. "We are all convinced of the benefits of herbal concoctions—and of your knowledge of them—now that sweet *Boppli* Elizabeth is crying less. Maybe you can teach me and Sarah a little about them."

Having come back to sit beside them, Sarah dropped to the freshly-turned garden furrow next to her *Mamm*. "Aren't you going home in the fall, Mercy? Will the plants grow big enough?"

"*Yah*. That's why most of these are seedlings that have already started to grow. My *Aenti* will have these here, even after I've gone home," Mercy smiled at the girl. "And most herbs and plants can be gathered from the woods nearby. I can teach you some basic recipes that use those."

The trio worked side by side in the garden next to *Onkle's* big barn without speaking, planting the tiny, delicate seedlings to make the tea for his aches and pains.

Finally, Kate said, "Hannah told me what a help you were at the farm stand, Mercy. I usually go along to help, but Elizabeth had a rough night before and we needed to make sure her naps were undisturbed."

"*Mamm*?" Sarah asked from the end of one garden row. "I finished this row, too. Can I go swing now? There is a big tree in front of the *Haus* that has a swing."

Mercy smiled. "Probably for *Onkle* and *Aenti's* grandchildren when they visit."

"Of course, *Liebling*. Take a break." Kate reached over to jiggle Elizabeth's chair where she sat in the sprouting green grass.

In a carefully-casual voice, Mercy said, "I saw Isaac at the farm stand."

"Did you?" Kate was bent over, poking her hand spade in the row. "He often sells his furniture there."

"I-I didn't know he built furniture. I knew he had a workshop, but not that he used it to actually build furniture. Hannah said he's quite good at it. He builds all kinds of things for folks around here."

"*Yah*. Good, sturdy furniture. He's working on a new bed for Elizabeth now." Kate sat back in the warm, sunny garden, pushing an escaped strand of black hair off her face. "He even said that an

Englischer furniture maker stopped by the farm stand, wanting to buy more things."

"All that must keep him busy if he has a farm to run, too." She didn't know how he managed it all and wondered if his farm was big.

In a suddenly teasing voice, Kate said, "You seem very interested in Isaac. He is a very good-looking *Mann*."

"What?" Mercy's head lifted. "No—"

She stopped, looking at her friend's mischievous smile. Did Kate know he'd come to her *Onkle's Haus*? Courtships were never announced or publicly addressed and all manner of flirtations were ignored until just before couples decided to marry, but of course, people knew. "Well, I do like Isaac. I mean, he's lots of fun."

The weight of her pretend courtship sank onto Mercy heavily. If he was supposed to be courting her, his family members at least would be aware of this. She hadn't considered that they'd be lying to anyone other than *Onkle* and *Aenti*. Mercy looked down at the dark garden soil, her eyes suddenly damp with regretful tears.

"Isaac's been such a flirt, although he's never really courted anyone for long." Kate continued planting before glancing up again. "I don't mean to upset you, Mercy—and we've never talked about this—but of course I'd heard that you were published to marry another *Mann* before. A *Mann* who left the Amish life before he married you."

The tone of Mercy's stifled "Yes" was due as much to her guilt as to the awkwardness of Daniel's actions. But of course she couldn't say that. It occurred to her to tell Kate that Isaac had only agreed to pretend to court her to get *Onkle* and *Aenti* off her back, but the words got stuck on her tongue. She certainly didn't want anyone thinking badly of Isaac for helping her with this.

She knew it might make them both look less than honest.

"I was to marry." Mercy looked down, saying, "Kate, do you remember Daniel? The *Mann* I was to marry? His last name is Stoltzfus. Daniel Stoltzfus. I believe he visited family here a year or two ago and you may have met him then. I hadn't realized it was here he came, but Isaac said Daniel had visited the Glicks."

Kate glanced over. "Isaac must have met him there. He was often at Abel Glick's workshop as a *youngie* and he and others helped *Frau* Glick with the farm as Abel grew more frail. Abel was the one who taught Isaac to make furniture. Oh, and many other things like those he sells at the roadside farm stand."

"Yes." Mercy self-consciously dug a finger into the moist newly-turned soil.

"Stoltzfus…" Kate meditated on the name. "Now that you mention it, I do believe the Glicks have some relations by that name."

"But, you don't remember Daniel?"

Ruefully, Kate shook her head. "I was a little…distracted these past few years. What with raising Sarah after Jakob died and then my *Eldre's* accident. I'm sorry, Mercy."

"*Neh*. Of course, I can imagine it must have been a very hard time for you." She didn't even know why she'd thought it was important to ask.

Her friend lifted a blue gaze to rest on Mercy's face. "You and this Daniel were already published to marry when he left? I don't think I ever actually knew his family name before."

"*Yah*." Mercy looked out at the peaceful farm yard, her unseeing gaze resting on the big barn. "I hadn't realized he was here until Isaac mentioned that he'd met Daniel that visit."

She shifted to send her friend a smile that felt shadowed, shivering all the sudden in the brisk spring air.

"Do you—do you miss him a lot now that he's gone?" Kate sent her a compassionate smile. "This Daniel?"

Pulling herself together, Mercy said honestly, "*Neh*. Not really. It sounds crazy, but I don't think so. Not him so much as— Well, the life we were to have together. I realized this since he left. You know, what you and Enoch have? A home and a family."

She made a face, saying with self-deprecation, "I just always thought I'd be married…and have *Bopplis* of my own."

The two women worked alone in the quiet garden, the silence that fell between them broken only by the sound of a bumble bee plundering the flowers nearby.

"I understand," Kate said finally. "When I married Jakob—my first husband—I thought we'd have a *familye* right off. But it was just Sarah, his child from an earlier marriage to a woman who'd died."

"That must have been upsetting," Mercy ventured.

Kate sat back again, stretching her back. "*Yah*, but I should never have married Jakob. It was a mistake. Enoch and I had courted...and I loved him. But we fought over me taking a *rumspringa* and—I don't know. We were stupid."

Giving spurt of laughter at her friend's words, Mercy smiled at her. "I have a hard time seeing you and Enoch as being stupid."

"Oh, we were." Kate shifted forward, smiling. "Really stupid. He'd say the same."

The other woman's candor made Mercy feel better admitting. "I guess I'm not sure I ever truly loved Daniel. I mean, if I had, shouldn't I miss him more? I mean, actually him? I think maybe I let things get as far as they did because, well, I got foolish about my *Mamm* and *Daed*. They didn't like Daniel much. Not really."

"No? And you were rebellious? Courting with a *Mann* your *Eldre* didn't like?"

"Yes." Mercy sighed, brushing her hands against one another after she dropped the last of her seedlings into the ground. "I thought I was all grown up. Everyone else was pairing up—you know how that goes—and I wanted to be settled, too."

"You and Daniel courted quite a while?"

"On and off for several years." Mercy shrugged. "It was...comfortable."

Her friend's smile was wry. "Until it wasn't?"

"Yes," Mercy admitted. "And now I'm tainted because the *Mann* I was to marry has left me...and our life. Just as many of our parents fear their children will do."

"And then you came here to Mannheim," Kate concluded. "Which was a good thing, I think."

"You are kind," Mercy smiled at her.

"And who knows?" Kate sent her a twinkling smile. "Maybe you'll be the reason Isaac finally settles down."

Murmuring something in reply, Mercy ducked her head in guilt. It didn't feel *gut* to lie to her friend.

Several days later, Isaac drove his rough field wagon up the track to Enoch and Kate's house, the new bed for *Boppli* Elizabeth in the back. Frowning as he gave the reins a gentle tug to stop the horse, he glanced at another buggy that was parked in front of the house, its horse lipping at the shoots of grass there. He hadn't expected that his *Bruder* and Kate might have other visitors.

"Hallo!" Enoch stepped out of the house, leaning on the porch rail there. "Come in!"

"Come help me," Isaac called "I have Elizabeth's new bed."

Isaac went to the rear of the farm wagon, lowering the back as Enoch came up. "Is this a bad time? Did I interrupt lunch with visitors?"

"Of course, not." Enoch leaned against the wagon as Isaac vaulted into the wagon bed. "Mercy is just here to help Kate gather some herbs from the garden."

Isaac lifted his brows. "Kate has herbs in her garden?"

"Apparently so. The *Mann* and his *Frau* that I bought the place from before they went to live with her children had planted some along the fence line. Mercy spotted it," his *Bruder* responded, reaching out to take hold of the small bed frame he scooted carefully toward the wagon back. "We just finished eating lunch and the women are out back in the garden. I thought it would be easier if I came in from the field to eat than to expect Kate to bring it to me. The *Boppli* takes her nap about now. Elizabeth's sleeping in the kitchen by the back door while Kate and Mercy forage in the garden."

His *Bruder's* house had a lovely peaceful feel, especially since little Elizabeth cried less.

Isaac slid his broad straw hat back on his head before lifting the other end of the bed frame.

"Oh! I thought I heard voices." Kate called out, appearing around the side of the house. Following behind her, Mercy joined them, carrying *Boppli* Elizabeth on her hip.

As always, her fair beauty caught at him and Isaac reminded himself—again—that *Gott* recommended looking on the inside. The more he got to know her, however, the more Isaac saw her inside as beautiful, too. It made him feel worse about having created the dark times through which she was now walking.

Even worse, although he felt bad about what he'd said to Daniel, Isaac couldn't regret that Mercy hadn't married.

In the flash of an instant, the dilemma swept over him. He'd prayed about his heedless words to Daniel. He'd never intended to have this consequence. And yet…here he was, mooning after the beautiful woman he'd injured. It was crazy and he felt sinful, being this attracted to her. But he was.

"Hey, *Schweschder*," Isaac shoved aside his troubled thoughts, greeting his sister-in-law as he caught the other end of the little bed Enoch carried. "Hello, little Lizzie!"

He made smoochy noises, aiming kisses at the *Boppli*.

Looking back at him with an unimpressed expression in her cherubic blue eyes, Elizabeth maintained her clutch on Mercy's sleeve, wisps of dark hair already growing below her tiny black *Kapp*. Isaac mentally bashed himself for envying the child being in her arms. He was crazy.

"And good day to you, Miss Mercy Yoder." He grinned at Mercy. Isaac couldn't help it. She just brought out the worst—best?—in him. "Did you wake *Boppli* Lizzie just now?"

Mercy couldn't help returning his smile. No longer surprised by the flush of warmth that streaked through her body at the sight of Isaac, she bounced the *Boppli* a little as she replied in a level voice, "Certainly not."

She'd never had this reaction to any *Mann* before, not even Daniel, and she must remember Isaac was only pretending to like her. This awareness of him was annoying.

"Elizabeth doesn't need anyone to wake her from naps." Kate said, smiling at her daughter. "But at least the colic has eased since we gave her the tea Mercy made."

Leaning over to tickle her daughter's cheek, she said, "See the wonderful new bed your *Onkle* Isaac made you, Elizabeth?"

"It is very nice," Mercy commented, scanning the bed frame as Isaac and Enoch carried it to the house. She was still startled that roguish Isaac had the patience to create such simple, beautiful furniture.

"*Denki*, kind lady," Isaac responded with a comical smirk, following his brother into the house with the bed.

Kate laughed, taking her *Dochder* from Mercy. "Isaac's a *Schaviut*. As the youngest of the *familye*, I guess being a rascal is only normal."

Following her friend to sit on a swing suspended on the wide porch as the men took the bed inside, Mercy sat down next to Kate.

"*Yah*, you are a wonderful *Boppli*." Kate smiled down at her *Dochder* who'd managed to free a small, fat, baby foot from her shoe and was now chewing on her toes.

Tilting her head as she smiled at Mercy, she asked, "You see the bed he made for Elizabeth, obviously. Did you get a chance see the other furniture Isaac makes when you helped Hannah the other day?"

"I did." Silently, Mercy chastised her heart for picking up its tempo at the thought of him. She'd just settled herself down from their short earlier exchange.

"As I said, he has a real knack for wood craft, Isaac does. Abel often commented on it when he was alive." Kate turned a question gaze toward her. "Do you know that Isaac has even had an *Englischer* furniture maker buy his chairs and table?"

Mercy wiggled the finger that *Boppli* Elizabeth had just grabbed, feeling her brows snap together. "*Neh*. I didn't know."

Kate shook her head as she stopped swinging, bending to retrieve the tiny shoe that had fallen from her lap. "He said an *Englischer* who manufactures furniture stopped at the stand—the week before last, I think—and left his card. It wasn't the first time the *Mann* had been by. The *Englischer* told Isaac he'd never seen as furniture so *gut*."

"This *Englischer* wants more of Isaac's furniture?" Mercy asked slowly as Kate again started the swing.

"On a regular basis? That would mean...living in the *Englischer* world, wouldn't it?"

"I don't know. I've never heard anything like that."

"Well, what did he say to this *Englischer*?" After the question left her mouth, Mercy realized her words had sounded sharper than she'd intended. She looked down, consciously calming herself before glancing up to meet Kate's gaze with a strained smile.

"I think he sold his furniture to the *Mann*, although he won't go, of course, if that were even suggested." Kate looked at her with kind eyes. "This Daniel you were to marry, he left to live in the *Englischer* world. *Yah*? You must be...upset by anyone doing the same."

Mercy's smile tightened. "Yes. I'm sorry I snapped at you."

"*Neh*, it's understandable that this would trouble you, but Isaac is a *gut* man. I've known the family a long time. I can't imagine Isaac turning from the way of *Gott*."

"Of course," Mercy hurried to say. "But you're right, his work with wood is exceptional."

Just then the sound of Isaac's joking voice could be heard approaching as he and Enoch came back out on the porch.

"So you were here to help Kate harvest herbs left by the Schraders? Herbs *Frau* Schrader must have planted?" Isaac perched on the porch rail opposite the swing, reaching out to tickle little Elizabeth's chin.

"*Yah*." Mercy found herself smiling as he stretched his arms out to Kate to take the *Boppli*.

The quickness with which her friend yielded up her little daughter to Isaac said a lot about how comfortable he was with the *Boppli*. He playfully lifted the child high like she was flying, cooing up at her.

It streaked across Mercy's awareness that an *Onkle* this loving couldn't easily leave his *familye*.

"I have heard," Isaac lowered the child to nestle her against his side, holding her with one arm, "that your herb tea has helped ease sweet Elizabeth's colic."

"It certainly has," Kate seconded from beside her on the swing that they moved forward and back in a gentle, unspoken rhythm.

He wiggled his eyebrows at Mercy. "I happen to know of a pasture filled with wild herbs."

Making a scoffing sound in her throat, she said, "Really? You know enough about herbs to recognize them?"

Isaac shrugged. "*Frau* Glick actually had some in her garden and she'd take me looking for them in the fields—when Abel was off delivering furniture he'd made."

Kate said in a teasing voice, "And you were how old back then? Yet, you claim to still recognize them?"

"I'm gifted that way," he responded in a modest tone.

The two girls laughed.

As Isaac stretched to hand the *Boppli* to her *Mamm*, he smiled down at Mercy. "How about you and I go tomorrow to look for the place I saw them? I could pick you up from your *Onkle's Haus*."

Even though she knew he was most likely playing the suitor role for Kate's benefit, Mercy found herself blushing. With her friend looking on benevolently, she smiled back at him and agreed. "That would be nice."

"What's in the bag?" Isaac asked as they drove away from *Onkle* and *Aenti's Haus* the next morning with Mercy's trim figure in his carriage next to him. Every time he saw her, it struck Isaac how beautiful she was with golden hair tucked under her black *Kapp* and her sparkling blue eyes. The plain green of her dress just set off her loveliness.

And she smelled good. Isaac had no idea what flowers she'd coaxed the scent out of, but there was no denying that Mercy smelled clean and sweet. Unable to resist, he took several quiet deep breaths, drawing her scent into his lungs.

He caught a glimpse of her *Aenti* looking at him stonily from a front window as they passed. Mercy's *familye* definitely wasn't fond of him, but he supposed that was her whole plan.

"This?" Mercy held up a small cloth bag as he started his buggy horse clip-clopping down the drive. "It's just something I brought in case I see Zacharius Graber again. I've crossed paths with him several times when out picking herbs. I thought we might run across him again today."

The days were growing warmer and as he directed the buggy down the Yoder drive, a pleasant breeze fluttered against them.

"I didn't know that old crab had even spoken to you." Clucking at his horse, Isaac turned the buggy onto the small road.

Lowering the bag to her lap, she said, "He hasn't. Much. I mean I did speak to him that day at the roadside farm stand, but that was it."

"And that was enough for you to make him—what?—some sort of herbal tea? Does he have colic like *Boppli* Elizabeth?" Isaac teased as his buggy horse trotted down the lane, his buggy rumbling after it. They passed fields of corn sheaves, reaching up to the blue sky in orderly rows and left Yoder land completely when he again turned the buggy onto another lane.

The scent of rotting radishes was strong here as an *Englischer* had heard that letting the crop decay in the fields helped the soil. Isaac wasn't sure of this, but since they passed the field, it didn't bother one used to the odor of manure.

"No," Mercy answered with a responding smile, "it's just...just some roots and herbs that might...might make him feel better."

Sitting next to her, Isaac slid her a questioning glance. "Old Zacharius Graber? Why would you want to make him feel better? I mean, him in particular."

The sound of the buggy horse's hooves filled the quiet before she responded. "He seems to need a pick-me-up."

"What he needs is intervention from *Gott*. He's mean as stink." Isaac glanced over at her again, enjoying the sight of Mercy beside him. "Although he does walk the fields since his *Frau* died, so we might well see him."

Mercy shook her head. "It must be very sad to have found love later in live and then for her to die."

"I suppose it is sadder than most. Zacharius Graber probably is sad, although he seems mad most of the time. Unless he's around Sarah and her friends. He seems nicer to *scholars*."

"That says a lot about him," she commented. "Some find *youngies* of that age to be very annoying."

She sounded kind and caring. Isaac suddenly found himself saying, "We could take the herbs to his *Haus* before we find the hidden herb fields, if you'd like."

His offer had nothing to do with annoying her *Onkle* or making up for his past transgression. He just thought it was important to her.

Mercy glanced over swiftly. "Can we? That would be wonderful."

"Of course. We're driving right by anyway."

"On the way to your secret herb fields?" She didn't seem to buy his claim.

"Well," Isaac laughed, "close enough."

Seeming to know he was making the stop just for her, Mercy appeared relieved that they reached the farm so quickly. From even before he'd directed the buggy into a bumpy, rutted drive, he noticed that the Graber land didn't seem to be in good condition. Fences needed mending here and there and the fields were fallow. The horse trotted up to a house that had peeling paint in front of a big barn that loomed over it. The entire place had a dilapidated air.

He'd had no idea the Graber farm had fallen into such a state. He and his *Daed* and *Bruder* should offer to help old man Graber fix it up.

When Isaac reined the buggy horse to a stop, Mercy placed a hand on his sleeve and he looked down at his arm, again feeling himself heat at her slightest touch even through the cotton of his shirt sleeve.

Apparently unaware of the fire she'd started in him, she said, "Stay here. I will only be a moment."

"Are you sure? I've never heard of Zacharius being more than mean, but I think I should probably go up to the door with you."

She gave him a confident smile. "I'm sure. I'll be right back."

Still a little doubtful, he murmured his agreement as she hopped out of the buggy, the horse now standing docile, the cloth sack in her hand. The Graber house rose up in front of them and she trod up the steps to knock firmly on a door that looked warped.

Isaac watched from his seat, tensing in readiness to spring to her assistance. It was silly. Graber had never been violent, even coming to the meetings despite talking with no one.

For several long minutes, there was nothing but the echo of her knock, as if the place were empty inside.

"Maybe he's out walking the fields," Isaac offered. Why this was so important to her was still a mystery to him.

Just when her trim green-clad figure had turned from the door, however, opened suddenly, shuddering a little as if not much used.

Zacharius Graber stood scowling in the doorway, hulking over her with his greater height. "What do you want?"

His gray head was bare of a hat and his sparse hair stood up in clumps while his beard looked unkept, as if he'd not brushed either in days.

"I brought you something, Mister Graber." Mercy held out the sack.

The old man stared at it for a minute, his face fierce with suspicion. "What? What is it? And why do you come here?"

"Because I thought this herbal mix might be good for you." She replied calmly.

Although he sat behind her in the buggy as she stood in front of Graber's door, Isaac could see her moving to loosen the sack opening.

"Look here, Mister Graber. See? It's an herbal mix for making tea that promotes good health."

Graber stared at her again. "Why would you care about my health?"

Isaac heard her say, "Isn't it *Gott's* will that we treat all with kindness?"

The elderly *Mann* standing still in his open doorway didn't challenge this, continuing to look at her fiercely.

"Make a tea of it, Mister Graber. It will be warm and comforting. We will look for you at the next Sunday services."

With those words, she turned and made her way down the rickety steps, back to Isaac's waiting buggy. He could see that the old *Mann* in the doorway now clutched Mercy's cloth bag in his gnarled hand, a frown on his face.

Reaching out for Isaac's extended hand, she climbed back into the buggy, saying to him serenely, "We can go now."

Her hand felt smooth, and warm and smaller and he'd had to remind himself let her go as she settled onto the seat beside him.

"Okaaay." Isaac turned to cluck at the horse, gently slapping the reins on its rump. The buggy started forward and they headed down Zacharius Graber's rutted drive, Mercy's trim figure next to him on the seat.

After a few minutes of silence, Isaac said, "How do you know he won't throw out the herbs? What makes you think he'll actually use them?"

"I don't know," she responded promptly. "But I must do my part. I leave the rest to *Gott*."

"I couldn't hear all you said. What did you tell Zacharius the herbs were for?"

"Good health."

Looking over at her, some shade in her tone made Isaac ask, "Is that all the herbs are for?"

"Is that not enough?" Mercy replied, turning her head to look at him with a level blue gaze.

He pulled the buggy to a stop as the lane joined another one, pausing while an *Englischer* car drove by. "You know it's enough, but I've started to get the impression, Mercy Yoder, that you're a woman who sometimes has motivations that aren't evident."

"You have." She looked down at her hands in her lap, pale against her darker dress skirt.

"*Yah*, I have." He clucked to start the horse again, turning on to the lane ahead.

She chuckled. "I have no clue as to what would give you that idea."

"Do those herbs you gave Zacharius have any other benefit?" He took his eyes off the road, to glance quickly her way.

"They have many." She didn't say anything more, but a little smile hovered around her mouth.

"Come on, Mercy. Out with it." Realization hit Isaac and he turned back to her. "You said several times that you think he's sad!"

"*Yah*, I do."

"You gave him something to make him less sad," he concluded, feeling triumphant that he'd figured out the puzzle.

Mercy giggled. "Good health makes a person feel better, doesn't it?"

"Absolutely," Isaac looked over again, "but I believe these herbs are specifically for getting a person to feel less sad. Come on, that's it, right?"

"Isaac, you don't even think Mister Graber will drink it," Mercy reminded him.

"He may not, but I'll bet he feels better if he does."

"I hope so. Just exactly where are those 'secret herb fields'?" she asked, changing the subject.

"Up here a ways. It's not far."

Mercy was glad he followed her lead. The tea might not change anything for Zacharius, but she had to do her part. Even though his *Frau* hadn't willingly left him, Mercy could understand that he might struggle to know how to respond to *Gott's* will.

The horse trotted on down the lane, twisting and turning until they approached a clump of trees beside a small covered bridge. It was a beautifully picturesque spot. Slowing to pull the buggy into a spot off the road, just beyond the bridge, Isaac looped the reins around the branches of a bush, making sure Ginger stood in a shady spot.

"Come, Miss Doubting Mercy. I'll show you where the best herbs grow."

A few moments later, she looked around, nothing about the glade dispelling her skepticism. In the distance, she could hear the burble of a brook. In the spring thaws, it probably turned into a noisy stream, thus the covered bridge.

"Do you not trust me?" he asked in mock outrage when she hesitated to take the hand he offered to help her off the buggy seat.

"Not entirely," she responded, her eyes narrowed as she placed her hand in his larger one and let him lead her from the buggy. The same *zap* she felt every time she touched him zinged through her and Mercy made herself laugh to cover her swiftly indrawn breath.

"Why, you are completely safe with me," Isaac assured her, his summer straw hat tipped back on his head as he walked toward the gully that ran beneath the bridge.

She wasn't so sure about that. It wasn't in the plan for her to enjoy him this much. Mercy said, as much for herself as for him, "I thought we were supposed to find a secret field of herbs."

"Oh, we are." He sent her his mischievous grin as he led her toward the heavily overgrown ravine. "Follow me. I just thought we might as well see the beauties of *Gott's* earth on our way."

"You know, if you wanted to be of help you could have just pulled weeds in the herb garden I've planted in my *Aenti's* plot." Mercy smirked as she carefully followed him down a narrow rocky path, the sound of running water growing louder. She was glad she'd put on shoes after working in the garden that morning.

"Yes, I could have," he agreed, "but then I'd have had to endure more of your *Onkle's* frowns and your *Aenti's* interruptions."

Aware that even by visiting with her, Isaac was doing her a favor, she didn't have a response to this. As they cleared the rocky path, the view opened up and she could see a lovely brook running over small boulders, the ripple of water filling the air with a musical babbling sound. Here and there, streams of sunlight broke through the trees above and the water sparkled in the light as it ran past.

"This is a beautiful spot." She halted, catching her breath as she took it all in. "You're right, this is one of *Gott's* glories."

A sandy patch of earth had been carved out by the brook and here and there she could see splotches of bright and dark green moss growing, looking like living velvet.

Having gone on ahead of her down the crescent-shaped sandy area, Isaac beckoned her forward as he lowered himself onto a bigger boulder by the water's edge. "Come on," he said, pulling at his shoes after he perched there. "Sit and we can let the water run over our toes."

She knew that by removing his shoes, Isaac would receive censure if the more critical congregation members—like her *Onkle*—saw him. Just then, however, she was feeling a little defiant herself. The brook looked cool and cheerful. As she lowered herself onto the boulder beside him, water lapped at the base of the stone. Next to her, Isaac was shrugging out of his jacket, his shirt white over broad shoulders, bisected by his suspenders.

Mercy ducked her head, trying not to notice—or feel the warmth of his body next to hers—as she reached beneath her skirts to remove her shoes.

"Go ahead," he urged, dropping his feet into the brook. "The water feels wonderful."

"You know," she said as she slipped bare feet into the chilly water, "you don't say big, flattering things about the herbs, like Daniel used to do."

Isaac looked over at her. "Did he? Well, I suppose he thought that was what you wanted to hear. Lots of girls like things like that."

"Don't you think" she stirred the cool water with her feet, "he would have known I didn't like that? After us courting for years."

"You courted for years?" Isaac paused and then lifted his hand, his broad palm upwards. "I'm sorry. I don't mean to pry."

She shrugged. "It's alright. No one talks to me about him. It's strange that they don't. Like he's died, only worse. Yes, we started courting when I was sixteen and Daniel was seventeen. Three years ago."

Making no reply, Isaac sat beside her in the idyllic spot.

Not upset by his quietness, Mercy said abruptly, "It may be wrong of me to say this—we were to be married after all—but I don't think I actually miss him. Not him, so much. I mean I liked him and all. I was startled to find myself saying this to Kate the other day."

Isaac drew a deep breath before saying carefully, "You don't miss him? But...this has to have been a hard thing. Being left like this."

"Yes. I liked Daniel fine. We'd always been together, you know?" She wiggled her feet, enjoying the sense of water running past. "But—but I think what I miss—the part I miss most is being—part of something. Having a place and a purpose."

He looked over at her again. "A place and a purpose?"

"You know." She lifted her shoulder, not sure how to explain it other than what she'd told Kate. "I expected that by now I would be a *Mann's Frau*. I'd work beside him and we'd have *Bopplis* to raise. This is what *Gott* created woman to do, is it not? To make a home and raise children? To offer comfort to her husband? What kind of woman am I that have no one to nurture? No harvest to help bring in."

"*Yah*." His response was slow. "I see what you're saying."

"I couldn't even get a husband." She knew she sounded glum and she felt ashamed of it.

He took off his broad straw hat and laid it to the side. "You've just been listening to your *Onkle* and *Aenti*. You'll get a husband when you're ready."

Isaac's immediate response lifted her spirits.

"Now come, Mercy Yoder. We have herb fields to see." He slipped off the rock to stand in the stream that lapped at his calves, holding his hand out for her.

"What?" she yelped. "I have to get into the water with you? Where are these herbs?"

"Just up the way," he said, leaning forward to take her hand. "This is why few have stumbled on it. We must walk across the creek."

Mercy shook her head, resisting the pull of his hand. "Are you crazy? My skirt will get all wet!"

"Hold it up, woman. Don't dither." He grabbed his shoes from the bank. He'd tied them together by the strings and hung them over his shoulder.

His face was so mock-serious that she, too, tied her shoe laces together and hung her shoes over her shoulder, gathering up her skirt in one hand as he tugged her into the water.

"Oh! My!" She gasped as the cold water lapped at her calves. It had felt refreshing on her feet, but now the water seemed icy, the bottom of the stream a mixture of sand and pebbles where she stood.

"We just have to cross here to find the most beautiful fields, filled with wild flowers and growing things. I don't think these fields have ever been planted." With his pants' legs rolled up over strong calves, he started plunking across the stream, still tugging her after him.

Beneath the noisily rushing water, Mercy's feet encountered chilly silty sand and firm rock places.

Suddenly, she hit a mossy patch, her arms windmilling. "Ohhh! *AAeeeeeee!*"

Free hand flapping as she desperately tried to regain her balance, she couldn't stop her slide. She flailed briefly, accepting fatalistically that the cold water of the stream would welcome her stretched out body when—

Isaac yanked hard on her hand, the hand he still held, jerking her up mid-fall.

"Are you all right?" He splashed back to her side. "That was close. What happened?"

"I-I h-hit a-a mossy p-place," she chattered out between suddenly shivering lips.

He put his arm around her to hold her up and she—already bombarded by the sensations of cold water and her near fall—was surrounded by his warmed and an alluring scent of his maleness. Mercy stood as the chilly wetness raced around her, acutely, overwhelmingly, transfixed by being in his arms.

"Come on, girlie. We need to get you to the other side."

Pain radiated up her ankle as he moved to guide her toward the other side. "*Ow, ow!* Isaac! My ankle!"

CHAPTER SIX

"Your ankle?" Standing knee deep in the surprisingly swift, cold water, Isaac held her still, his arm around her trim waist to balance her. He was particularly glad of that when he felt her falter as she tried again to set her ankle on the squishy river bottom.

Mercy gasped. "Yes, I must have sprained it when I stumbled just now."

He turned around more fully, staring in dismay. "Are you sure?"

"No, Isaac." Her voice was suddenly waspish as she wobbled in the water. "I'm pretending because I think it's a fun joke."

Staring at her in growing alarm, he ignored her sarcasm, moving a little closer to steady her.

"We must get out of this water," he said decisively, aware of his bare feet growing numb with the cold. "Can you walk on it at all?"

"No," she said in a voice that quavered, "and the bottom of my skirt has fallen into the creek water. It's all wet!"

"Here." Isaac turned around, squatting into the chilly water. "Climb on my back."

Mercy yelped, "What!"

"It's the only way to get you out of the stream since your ankle can't bear your weight. Come on, I'm freezing here."

"Climb on your back?"

He heard the scandalized note in her voice, but was also aware that she had a firm grasp of his suspenders.

"Yes," he urged. "Here. Take my hand and I'll use the other to boost you up."

They must have made a wobbly, comical sight—him bent to accommodate her smaller stature, her hopping forward through the water on one leg. The cold, rushing water tugged at his chilled calves and he tried to focus on that instead of the fact that an extremely shapely woman was hoisting herself onto his back.

Almost instinctively, he reached with one hand to grab her as he lifted her with his other hand.

"*Aaeeiee!*" Mercy squealed as he pulled her onto his back, shifting her weight up higher.

"Put your arms around my neck. Go on!"

Finally, she did as he directed, shifting her hands from where she clung to his shoulders to securely attach them together under his chin.

He stood in the stream then, hesitating briefly with the weight added to his back, thinking how best to maneuver them without dropping her. In a quick flash, he considered the choices. He could grasp her arms—now thrown around his neck—but that would leave the length of her draped over his back, legs dangling in the water. If she'd been his young niece, Sarah, he'd have used his hands to push her bottom higher, so he could carry her more safely.

That was not an option with Mercy.

Just the thought of touching her in that way made the water around him seem a lot warmer. Knowing the situation called for prudence, he asked carefully, "Can you put your knees around me?"

She didn't answer for a moment.

"I can grip you more securely," he explained, "if you straddle me."

"Oh-h." Her teeth still chattered as she wiggled around.

He assumed—since he doubted she was trying to drive him out of his mind—that she was freeing her legs from her long skirts.

After a moment, Isaac felt her shift her knees forward on either side of his waist and he quickly slipped his arms under each leg, hooking them over his arms. Grasping his own hands together, he leaned forward to counter her weight on his back. "Let's go. We've got to get out of this water. It's your right ankle?"

"*Yah.*"

Doubting she wanted to hear at that moment how good she felt against him, he began moving back toward the river edge from which they'd started.

"Just hold on to me," he recommended, sloshing through the water.

"You know-w," she chattered the words into his ear in an almost conversational tone as he slogged toward the stream's edge with her on his back, "if any member of the church were to see us—"

"I know," he interrupted as he approached land, "I should just leave you here. In the cold water, with a sprained ankle. Besides, we can't be seen from any road."

That silenced her for a moment as he waded forward, telling himself that a *Mann* of *Gott* shouldn't be so aware of the shape of her body pressed against his back. He felt her womanliness and knew he shouldn't. Even wet, she wasn't heavy and he felt he could carry her forever.

Finally reaching the sandy shore, Isaac staggered out of the water, arms still clenched to his side to hold her up. His feet and legs chilled, he stood on the warmer sandy dirt, welcoming the absence of the cold water. After a moment, he looked around. Here and there, clumps of grass and moss dotted the small clearing beside the creek, spangled with blotches of sunlight. Darkening green leaves adorned the maple and ash trees around them, now that summer was fully on them.

"Can you stand on your good leg if I set you down?" He felt warmer just having gotten out of the chilly stream. Isaac took several steps into a patch of sunlight through the tree branches.

"*Yah.* I think I can." Her voice wavered a little as he lowered her next to a fallen tree.

Isaac held on to her hand as she sank gracefully to the ground. "Here, let me look at your ankle."

Pushing aside the sodden edge of her green skirt, he bared her wet, swollen foot, touching it gently to check for obvious broken bones. "Does this hurt?"

"A little. More if you pressed harder."

He smiled at her. "Don't worry, I'm not pressing harder."

Spreading her wet skirt out on either side of her, Mercy said, "It's warmer here in the sun."

"Maybe we'll dry off some if we sit here a while." He sprawled next to her in the sunny patch.

She pulled her skirts out more fully. The silence that fell between them was filled by the noisy stream and the sound of calling birds, high in the trees.

Letting the peace of the place seep into him, Isaac again wondered how anyone could doubt the existence of *Gott*. A spot like this was a gift in a turbulent world. He drew a deep breath, feeling humbled and unworthy.

"I'm sorry, Mercy. This is all my fault." Isaac hadn't planned his apology. It spilled out of him without conscious forethought. He should never have tried to cross the stream with her. He added ruefully, "My *Daed* and *Bruders* would say this was just another case of Isaac being impulsive and not thinking things through."

"They would?" She fiddled with her drying skirt.

"*Yah*. I'm the family *Schaviut*," Isaac admitted. "Always into some crazy, rascal thing or another."

The thought streaked through him that she didn't know the half of it.

Mercy looked over at him, her gaze considering.

"They always seem so *gut* and so harmless, my ideas." He shrugged. The possibility that Daniel—although Isaac hadn't liked him—would go so far as to end his engagement and leave their life altogether had never even occurred to him.

"This is not so bad," she said finally.

Startled, Isaac stared at her. "You must be joking. Your *Onkle* and *Aenti* would say this is the very kind of trouble they knew I'd lead you into."

She shrugged. "Perhaps, but we need to look at this reasonably. No one was killed. I've sprained my ankle, but nothing really terrible happened."

That she would take such a practical attitude in a moment like this had never occurred to him.

"Don't look so startled." She reached out to her drying skirt to pull a damp spot more fully into the light.

"I'm just surprised," he admitted. "This is not what most girls would say."

"Probably not." Her voice was matter-of-fact. "You know what, Isaac? I think you act all cocky and rascally, but down deep you're less sure of yourself than you look."

Isaac drew another deep breath. It was as if she'd read his insides.

"Not that you're prideful or boastful or anything—except maybe when playing volley ball—but you look always sure of yourself." Her gaze was considering.

Holding her look for a few moments, before he knew it, Isaac leaned forward and pressed his mouth against hers.

Mercy seemed to go still, not pulling back, her mouth moving ever so gently against his. She smelled of summer flowers, sweet and subtle. After only a moment, she pulled back, her warm blue gaze locked on his.

Eventually he looked down, picking at the stubby grass between his legs. He knew he shouldn't have kissed her and knowing that, wasn't sure why he had. "You're right, Mercy Yoder. I'm not always sure of myself. I didn't know I looked so sure of myself."

Mercy smiled at him then and it seemed she wasn't going to refer to their brief kiss. "It's mostly when you're teasing and being silly. Are you ready to climb back up to the buggy? I think my skirt's pretty much dry now."

Glad of her transition away from the loaded moment, Isaac asked, "It is?"

He patted his pants' legs. "*Yah*. I'm drying, too."

She scooted into a more upright position, scrambling to her one good foot. "Turn your back so I can climb aboard."

Isaac laughed. "Yes, indeed. I'll be your buggy horse."

Half an hour later, Isaac pulled the reins to stop his buggy in front of the Yoder *Haus*. "How do you want to do this? You don't need to put any weight on that ankle."

"No." She considered the house and nearby garden, looking up the steps to the front porch. "No one appears to be around."

He climbed down looping the reins around a nearby tree branch. "Come. I'll carry you up the steps. I don't think you should try to mount them, but you could hobble inside, if that seems safer."

"Okay." She looked down, her smooth face not showing anything but concentration as she shifted forward on the buggy seat. "Isaac, I don't think we should say anything about the stream to *Onkle* and *Aenti*. They already don't like you and I don't want you having to deal with any more from them."

Her gaze flashed up to his and her voice softened. "You're doing me this wonderful favor, pretending to court me to get them to back off."

"It's no hardship for me, Mercy," he admitted, thinking that he shouldn't enjoy his penance so much. Maybe this was more than an atonement. Maybe *Gott* had thrown him and Mercy together. He could only hope that was true.

"*Denki*." She laughed, reaching out a hand to balance on his shoulder. "I keep forgetting you're used to being such a *Schaviut*. This pretense is actually fun for you."

Isaac reached out, scooping her up in his arms. Her weight was light and he tried mightily not to notice how sweetly her curves pressed against him, his memory filled with thoughts of her mouth beneath his. "You're right. Maybe I shouldn't be, but I am having fun."

Several days later, a male *Englischer* voice stopped Mercy in her tracks before she walked up behind Isaac's furniture booth. She was again helping Hannah at the roadside farm stand and had taken a break since produce customers were sparse. Her ankle was much better, leaving her only favoring it a little. She didn't think she should feel this way, but the sprain seemed small in comparison to the fun she'd had. Although it shouldn't have, the memory of the kiss she'd shared with Isaac and of his sincere voice had filled too many of her thoughts since their afternoon seeking hidden herb fields.

"Really, Isaac," the *Englischer* spoke again. "Your stuff is great. I need a designer just like you since my other guy just retired."

"*Denki*, Mr. Abbott. And you want these other chairs? You've already bought several of my chairs and tables—" Isaac's voice was deeper than the *Englischer's*.

Mercy held her breath, standing paused on the path that ran behind the farm stand booths, her view of Isaac's booth blocked by the thin wooden partition on the sides and at the back of the booths. She knew she should walk away. This certainly wasn't her business.

Suddenly, she felt shaken and stumbled back against the booth frame. Was this the *Englischer* Kate had spoken about?

Isaac had agreed to their pretend courtship to annoy her *Onkle*...like she'd wanted to do. Only now she kept thinking of Isaac beyond that. Thinking of him in ways that had nothing to do with *Onkle* Yoder.

The *Englischer* spoke again. "Yes, I've bought several things and everyone raved at their simplicity and beauty, Isaac. You have a real gift. Here's payment."

Mercy heard the shuffle of paper, as if money was changing hands.

The *Englisher* said. "Seriously, Isaac. If you're ever looking for job doing just this, I'd be very glad to hire you as one of my workers. You'd have to live closer to the factory, of course."

The *Englischer* laughed.

From her spot behind the booth, Mercy froze, hearing Isaac laugh in response. *"Denki* again for the purchase, but I'm not looking for more jobs. I'm not sure how I'd even manage having more to do. Let me help you take these things to your car."

It flashed all over her that the *Englischer* was presenting Isaac with a job outside their world. Just as she feared when Kate had spoken about the man. He wanted to get Isaac to leave Mannheim…like Daniel had left Elizabethtown.

Mercy heard the *Englischer* respond faintly as his and Isaac's voices receded.

She stood with her back against the booth, a sudden rush of heat flooding her body as a ringing grew in her ears. This *Englisher* would hire Isaac to work for him. In another town.

It was as she'd feared.

Until that moment Mercy didn't realize just how much Isaac was beginning to mean to her. Not fully.

And he now had very solid temptation to leave their world.

Two days later, Mercy sat in the late afternoon light under the big catalpa tree in *Aenti's* backyard, scrubbing at a stubborn stain on her next best dress. Sunday meeting was the next day and as always she wanted to look tidy and presentable. The rasping of katydids had already started as the afternoon gently faded into twilight.

Although she didn't want to, she'd found herself thinking a lot about Isaac and the *Englischer's* proposition. It shouldn't matter to her. He'd made her no true promises and it wasn't unheard of for *youngies* to leave their life. Of course, Isaac wasn't exactly a *youngie* anymore. He was a *Mann* and he'd already joined the church.

Of course, so had Daniel.

She again slapped the dress down on the scrubbing board. It was nothing to her, she reminded herself fiercely. Nothing.

Psst!

Of course, it would crush Samuel, Enoch, Kate and even little Sarah if Isaac left. Probably the rest of the community, too.

Psst!

Making a sour face at the wash basin, Mercy thought Isaac might leave others behind, hearts fainting at the thought of him shunned and gone beyond their reach. Girls who had hopes where he was concerned. Probably lots of girls.

Psst!!!

Mercy glanced up, jerked from her thoughts as the sound finally intruded. Looking around, she didn't first see anyone in the shadow of the barn.

"Mercy!" A familiar voice called in hushed tones. "Over here."

To her shock, her former fiancé, Daniel Stoltzfus, stood in the shadow at the corner of the large building, beckoning her over.

A thousand thoughts streaked through her brain, her heart making a stuttered jump. Daniel? Here?

Dropping the wet dress into the bucket, she rose to her feet and looked at where he stood. His tall figure was so familiar as he waited in the shadows. She could see that his pants were dusty and his head bare.

Daniel was shunned now that he'd rejected *Gott*. The entire community had voted it. No Amish person was to speak to him.

Her head whirling, she turned her back on the shadowed spot where he stood. He was shunned.

"Come here!" he hissed again

As if compelled, Mercy glanced back to see him gesturing to her more urgently.

On feet that moved as though weighted, she crossed the yard, stopping before she reached him. How could she stand closer? "Daniel."

"Yes. It's *gut* to see you, Mercy."

She could see the muscles in his throat move as he swallowed. "I must speak to you."

Remaining a yard away from him, she said, "You know I cannot speak to you, Daniel. You assured that by leaving the church."

Before he could answer, she found herself asking, "How did you know I was here?"

He looked thinner and worn, as if in taking such a drastic step as leaving his life—their world—he'd aged.

He swallowed again, "I overheard Micah and Levi talking about you having come to stay with your *Onkle* and *Aenti* Yoder."

"My brothers spoke to you?" The last she'd heard all five of her brothers had threatened to do him harm. Not that they would disobey *Gott* in that way.

Even in the shadowed twilight, she could see him flush, his features clouding. "*Neh.* I didn't speak with them, but—but when I stood where I thought you might pass, I—I overheard them talking."

"Your *Mamm* and *Daed* are well last I knew," she said deliberately, watching him color again.

"*Gut.*" He motioned toward her again. "Won't you come closer, Mercy?"

"Why are you here, Daniel?" She didn't move, still not trusting him. Hating the familiar sense of this, the accustomed feel of being with him that settled over her like a blanket. He'd been her childhood friend. The first boy to ever walk her home after a Sing. She'd planned to marry this *Mann*, to stand before *Gott* and all their friends, promising to stay by his side no matter what. It made no sense given his actions, but she still felt fondness for him all mixed up with her anger. After all, it was due to his betrayal that she was now tainted goods.

"I've missed you, Mercy." He looked a little more ragtag than she remembered, but his eyes were the same blue and the sight of him was sweeter than she'd expected. "Are you *gut*?"

She said with difficulty. "*Yah*, I am fine. I-I mean, it has been difficult...since you left."

"I'm sorry." He looked down. "I didn't mean to hurt you. I hope you know that."

Mercy looked at him for a long moment. She didn't know what to believe about his intent. He'd never been less than kind before, maybe a little unaware, but not unkind. He'd not won the games or flirted with all the girls, but she'd often told herself that this was a *gut* thing. What woman wanted a *Mann* who philandered with other girls?

"I suppose I've missed you, too, Daniel," she said slowly. "In between praying to *Gott* to forgive me for hating you."

It occurred to her to ask if he'd seen his *Mamm* and *Daed*, but she stopped, knowing nothing would be the same. Even his *Eldre* wouldn't speak to him, not since he'd been shunned. "At least, I've had random thoughts of missing you until it hits me again that you broke off our engagement and left this life."

He reached out of his shadowed spot, grasping her hand to pull her next to him in the darkness clustering around the barn. "I sorry about all that. I came for you, Mercy. That's why I'm here. To get you."

"What?" She jerked her hand free of his touch, knowing her voice was stunned.

"To get you. To take you with me." He spoke with an almost feverish intensity. "You can come with me and we'll make this life together. We've always been together."

"Mercy! Mercy!" Her *Aenti* suddenly appeared on the house's back porch, calling her name as she peered around the yard. "Are you here?"

"We can go together." Daniel whispered, reaching out to draw her closer as if to hide from her *Aenti's* gaze.

Up next to him, she drew in his familiar smell and tried to ignore the shaking in her stomach. The back door bounced shut as her *Aenti* went back inside, apparently satisfied that Mercy wasn't in the yard any longer.

"Daniel." She tugged loose from his hold. "I-I am sorry, but I don't think I want to go with you, to leave this life."

He looked stunned.

"*Neh*, I know I don't want to go with you." Her heard beat rapidly in her chest. "I'm sorry."

"You just haven't thought about this," he said, almost as if reassuring himself, recapturing her hand in his again. "This is all new to you. But there is this amazing world out there—"

She interrupted him. "*Neh*, Daniel. I have thought about it. I love *Gott*. I love this life."

He looked affronted. "I love *Gott*, too, Mercy. You mistake the entire *Englischer* world. There are many churches. Many preachers making sermons. The Amish are not the only ones who love *Gott*."

"Perhaps not," she took a step back. "But this is how I worship, Daniel. Here. This is my Godly life. I have no interest in leaving it. I can't talk longer. I must go in to my *Aenti* now."

The deep grass swished against Mercy's skirt the Monday after Sunday service as she walked across the fields. Earlier she'd helped her *Aenti* bake the week's bread and start lunch for the men working in the Yoder fields. She'd earned some time to wander collecting herbs and flowers...and to think about her realization that she cared more for Isaac than she'd realized....

And now *Englischer* was trying to tempt him into that world. The thought made her sick.

She couldn't help think also about Daniel's secretive visit and his strange invitation. She'd spoken with him, even though she knew she shouldn't, even though he was shunned.

She had no interest in leaving her world, but seeing Daniel again had been...strangely *gut*. Glad to have slipped away into her peaceful place, she tramped along, ever watchful eyes on the plants growing along her path, puzzling and concerned about Daniel.

The situation with Isaac hadn't yet developed as she feared it might, but Daniel had certainly appeared in solid form.

Having fully risen now, the sun shone down strongly on her *Kapp*-covered head and shoulders as she walked through the fields. By this time, she knew well the pastures around the Yoder farm house and had roamed often into the nearby farmland. Mercy clambered over a stile into the next field. The furrows there were crowned with rows of sprouting green.

Crossing the open space, she headed for the field edge, a fringe of smaller trees and shrubs trickling down into a valley. Bees bumbled over the rows, intent on their prize, as she crossed to the far side of the pasture.

Under one of the taller trees, she suddenly saw Isaac, his broad hat tilted back, a smile on his handsome face. "Hello to you, Mercy. I hoped you might walk this way."

Dangerously glad to see him, she continued past where he waited and fell in step beside her. Spending time with Isaac drew her mind away from places she'd rather not continue dwelling on. As he walked alongside her, matching her steps, she cast him a gently mocking sideways glance. "Do you never work your field, Isaac?"

His grin glinted at her. "*Maedel*, I rose before the sun, finished my tasks there and spent some time in my workshop."

Registering the muscular breath of him as he walked casually next to her with an easy, well-built smoothness, she said, "I am hardly a young girl, Isaac."

He made a scoffing sound in his throat. "You're just a sprout."

A chuckle broke free of her. "A sprout?"

"*Yah*, just a young woman on the cusp of being grown up."

Mercy shook her head, smiling.

"I have," he said, smiling at her with a glint in his eye as he reached out for her hand, "thought a lot about that kiss, Miss Mercy. Have you?"

Again tingling at his touch as her fingers curled around his, she nervously put her other hand up to her *Kapp*, although it was pinned in place. Hesitating briefly, she admitted, "I have."

"It was very pleasant," he said. "Very."

"Do not try to convince me, Isaac, that you've not kissed many a *Maedel*." Although her heart beat faster, she threw him a deliberately teasing glance as they continued hand-in-hand through the tall grass in the next field, "

"I have kissed some," he admitted, "although not as many as you probably think."

Raising skeptical brows, Mercy had to acknowledge to herself, another smile spreading over her face, that she was glad he'd waited here for her. She might not know for sure that he, too, wouldn't disappear on her, but she really...enjoyed his company. "You told me yourself that you're a *Schaviut*."

"I have been." He continued walking alongside her holding her hand, now looking down at the ground his feet trod. He cleared his throat. "But I have not enjoyed kissing anyone as much as you, Mercy."

His words were said with such sincerity her steps faltered as she glanced over at him. She didn't know how to respond to this, aware that the buzzing in her body now seemed to spread like sap in a springtime tree.

"I think," Isaac and she stood facing one another in the blowing grass, hands clasped, "I think I want to court for real, Mercy. No pretend. I want to truly court you."

Her throat felt dry and she had to clear it before trying a lighthearted note. "You think?"

Isaac nodded, saying in a voice that had no teasing in it, "*Yah*, I do. Will you court with me?"

She started walking again, her steps slow as they were still tethered by the grasp of his hand and hers. He walked alongside her again.

How could this kind of situation be again placed in front of her? What was *Gott* trying to tell her? Was this even-greater heart risk with Isaac a punishment for her feelings about Daniel leaving? She hadn't ever believed *Gott* was cruel.

"I know you were hurt when Daniel left," Isaac said, "and you're not looking for a *Mann* now, but I hope you have enjoyed being with me as I have enjoyed being with you."

It was hard for her to believe what she heard, but an undeniable lightness seemed to have flooded her whole body. To her dismay, she realized she wanted to believe him...even though she thought she shouldn't. Even though this might scar her more than she'd ever been before.

Mercy smiled up at him, trying to keep the conversation lighthearted. "This is more of your teasing. How could any girl believe these words from a *Schaviut* like you?"

"I am totally sincere. No teasing." He sent her a faint, answering smile. "Will you think about it at least?"

She hesitated before responding with a candid smile. "Isaac, it's hard for any girl not to think about it when a *Mann* says he wants to court her. Even if she's not sure he's sincere."

His expression grew more serious. "I'm not teasing at all. I mean every word. And to make sure you keep thinking of me, Mercy, I am going to kiss you again. I've been longing to do so since our last kiss.

Without question, she could have moved away, dodging his caress, but she didn't. She'd been thinking of their kiss, too.

He dipped his head and the broad brim of his hat cast shade over her face just as his mouth coasted on to hers. Feeling the sizzle of their melded mouths, she sank against his powerful body, surrounded by the clean, warm male scent of him.

When the kiss ended, Isaac said, "Continue keeping company with me. Let me convince you that I'm serious."

She did move away then despite the buzzing in her veins. As she did so, she said back over her shoulder, "Well, if I'm to avoid *Onkle* and *Aenti's* constant matchmaking, we should probably continue seeing one another."

CHAPTER SEVEN

A week later, Isaac stood in front of his work bench, the *shush* of his plane glided over the wood. His hands following a familiar, trained pattern, he smoothed the lumber, the smell of fresh wood shavings floating around him...his head filled with thoughts of Mercy. His shop was always his thinking place. Wood coming alive beneath his hands seemed to free his mind.

In the time since they'd agreed to pretend to court, he'd seen her almost every day. Even having to see sour puss Hiram Yoder hadn't kept him from her smiles and the warm, smooth touch of her hand.

The summer day was a warm one, the sounds of buzzing insects in the yard outside joining with the hush of his wood plane. Isaac smiled to himself, his blood running warm inside him at the thought of Mercy's laughter and the tilt of her blonde head. Even the sardonic roll of her eyes in response to one of his teasing remarks just made him want to spend more time with her. Just thinking of her returning to her *Eldre's* home in Elizabethtown made him feel empty inside. He wondered what his life would be like when she left.

It still startled him to realize he couldn't see a life for himself without Mercy.

No other girl had fit into his world so well. He hadn't wanted more time with the other girls, hadn't fallen into daydreams of them in their absence. He didn't know what it was about this woman, but she seemed to have turned everything in him upside down. One blonde-haired girl seeking refuge from a broken engagement had gotten under his skin and he was actually moving toward plighting his troth to her before *Gott*.

If she'd have him.

From nearly the first when she'd helped poor Sarah to later when she'd offered the elixir that helped *Boppli* Elizabeth's colic, to her interest in easing Zachariah Graber's pain, he saw that she was a good, loving woman. It didn't hurt that he often wanted to catch her in his arms and kiss her until she clung to him and breathed his name.

Many of the *Maedels* he'd grown up with were nice girls and he'd always expected that he would have eventually settled down with one of them…if he hadn't met Mercy. They all now seemed as if some spice was missing, though. He'd never thought he wanted a woman who could give him sass occasionally.

He liked Mercy's spunk. She wasn't the kind of woman it would be easy to put something over on.

The thought of her and Daniel together made no sense…and it was even more vital that she never learn of the role he'd played in her former betrothed's departure from the Amish life.

He felt the urge to confess everything to her, but the possibility that she'd turn from him in disgust kept him silent.

"May *Gott* go with you and help you live a plain and simple life." Bishop Yoder ended the service the next Sunday, nodding toward Mr. Schneider who owned the house in which they met.

As people began milling around after the sermon ended, Mercy glanced over where Zacharius Graber sat. It had been some days since she and Isaac had dropped off the cloth bag with ginko biloba at his *Haus* on the way to their ill-fated creek wading episode. Her ankle felt much better now, but she couldn't help wondering about Mr. Graber.

Of course between Isaac's unexpected declaration that he truly wanted to court her...and her secretive visit from Daniel...she hadn't had a lot of time to think about the old *Mann*.

She got up now to join the other women preparing lunch in the kitchen, knowing her help would be gratefully accepted. As she slipped through the crowded room, Mercy sliced a glance toward Zacharius.

It just so happened that he looked up then, his gaze meeting hers. Mercy deliberately smiled at him. It might seem like the decades difference in their ages and the lack of any connection outside of Sunday services would mean they had little in common, but she felt a linking together with him that few would understand.

They were both suffering from the departure of those they'd loved...or in her case, counted on. They were both now alone.

Even if she'd come to realize that Daniel wasn't her only option as a mate, she still understood Zacharius' loss. When Daniel left, he'd taken a whole life away from her. A life she'd expected him to share.

Although Mr. Graber held her gaze for a moment, he didn't return her smile. She felt some relief that he didn't scowl more heavily at her—after all she'd intruded herself into his world—but his face didn't beckon her forward, either.

Heading over to the hot kitchen area, she worked alongside the other young women to feed the group. The warmth inside the house only grew as second and third lunch seatings took place, since there wasn't room at the tables for all at once.

After the last bunch was served the rooms finally cleared out and Mercy finished a soapy sink of dirty dishes before taking her own plate full of food. Going out to the wide porch where clusters of folk stood chatting and cooler breezes fanned her hot face, she went down the steps with her plate, looking for a cool spot to settle.

Off to the side, seated alone under the shade of a big old oak tree was old Zacharius. He seemed aloof, holding his now-empty plate in his gnarled hand as he stared ahead, seemingly at nothing in particular.

Mercy swallowed, pausing in the yard in front of the *Haus*. She could seek a shady spot near one of the other girls from the kitchen, eating their dinners after feeding the others, or she could find her friends Kate and Hannah...or Isaac. She wavered, standing there looking at Zacharius, feeling a tugging that made no sense.

Maybe *Gott* was nudging her. She didn't know, but she found herself moving across the yard toward the tree where Zacharius sat. It bothered her to see his lonely, angry face.

"Mr. Graber," she paused as the shadow of the big tree fell across her face, "may I sit here under the tree with you?"

The older *Mann* turned to look at her, his gaze shooting over to apparently survey the clusters of people in the farm yard. When he glanced back at her, his regard was faintly suspicious. He nodded finally, though. "Sit wherever you please, *Maedel*."

"*Denki*," she replied, stepping forward to a gnarled, raised root next to him under the tree. Sinking to the ground, with her navy skirt billowing slightly as she sat, Mercy settled at foot or so from the old man.

They ate in silence, separated from the others—him chewing still on a chunk of bread—while she quietly consumed her lunch. Light summer breezes stirred the air every once in a while and outside the shade of the tree, the sun shone bright. Finally, she asked quietly "Does the tea from the root I gave you upset your stomach?"

He turned to stare at her before responding, "*Neh*. Is that what the root mix you gave me is for? To make me sick? I've not used it."

Laughing, she said, "No. I'm not trying to poison you or make your life worse. It's—it's to make you—feel stronger. Less tired."

"*Maedel*, why would you think I feel tired?" His quick response was clipped and a shade angry.

Having spooned in another mouthful, she took a moment to chew and swallow before responding. "Don't you?"

She had no wish to irritate or enrage him. Not wanting to give offense, Mercy added, "I just thought you might."

Zacharius glared at her before finally admitting, "There are times I do. It's natural for a *Mann* of my years."

She looked down at her half-eaten plate of food, remembering Daniel's face in the shadow of the barn...and remembering Isaac's kiss. "Mr. Graber, it's natural to us all to feel tired at times."

The old man made a scoffing sound in his throat. "What would a *Maedel* like you know about it?"

Mercy found herself staring at him. Before she realized it, she blurted out, "Do you not know why I am here, Mr. Graber? Has no one told you about me?"

She got the impression that she'd startled him, noticing that he squinted an eye in her direction. "Told me what about you? I'm not one to listen to gossip? Why would anyone have spoken about you?"

His voice was rough, as if he couldn't imagine someone else having as big a burden as he.

Mercy cleared her throat, almost wishing she'd said nothing. "You may have noticed that I sit in service with my *Aenti* Yoder."

"*Yah*. What of it?"

Her brows lifted, she asked in a lightly self-mocking voice, "Have you never heard of the Bishop Yoder's *Bruder* and his "princess" daughter? The youngest in the family and the only *Maedel*?"

Something that looked like realization dawned on his craggy face. "Then...you are...?"

"And haven't you heard," she continued ruthlessly, "about that girl being ditched by the *Mann* she was to wed? Only days before the ceremony? And that Daniel—the *Mann* I was to marry—left the life?"

Mr. Graber took another bite of bread, jerking it off the hunk in his hand and chewing in silence before he swallowed. His words then were both roughly dismissive...and strangely comforting, "If others were tittle tattling about such, I didn't attend."

"Well," Mercy commented with the sudden realization that he spoke the truth, "it doesn't matter. My—my loss is nothing to yours."

Again, Zacharius Graber looked at her for a long moment. "You've been listening to tittle tattle yourself, haven't you, *Maedel*?"

"I don't think so." She smiled at him kindly.

His craggy face grew more stern and he fell silent.

Mercy cleared her throat. "I—I can't imagine—finding such a love as you did—only to lose it."

"Is it not the same with you?" Graber's words were shaded with aggression.

She didn't feel threatened, though. Acknowledging sadly to herself again that the dissolution of her relationship with Daniel had shaken her plans for her future, but not necessarily her heart, she uneasily turned toward her lunch companion.

"You've heard that I was to marry, but this loss still cannot measure against yours."

Zacharias picked up an apple that had sat on his plate, rubbing it against his pant knee. "*Neh*. Maybe, but it is still hard for you."

"Yes." She fiddled with the fork on her plate, looking up at him suddenly.

"I—I have not mentioned it to anyone—" she hesitated for a moment, but the urge to confide in a disinterested, objective ear was strong. To have such a conversation with him seemed unreal, but she could be sure that Zacharius Graber wouldn't gossip about her stealthy conversation, "I may have— Daniel came to see me just this past week. In secret. And I spoke with him."

"Is this *Mann* not shunned?" Zacharius looked as always, his expression harsh, but not judgmental.

"*Yah*," she said, grimacing at him. "This is why he came where no one could see him."

The older *Mann* crunched into the red fruit, his expression not changing.

She shook her head. "He wants me to go with him, to leave our life and marry him."

After chewing a moment, Zacharius asked, "What do you want?"

It seemed strange and peculiar to be talking like this…with him of all people. She certainly wouldn't have expected it.

"I said I didn't want to leave my life here, that I worship *Gott* by living this plain, simple life. I really have no interest in the *Englischer* world."

"But his visit and his invitation for you to join him still troubles you," the old man said shrewdly.

Mercy stared at him. "Yes. I think…I am most upset about my lack of grieving him. I—I should feel something more. I should have missed him more—himself, I mean. Shouldn't I? Maybe I…can't really love anyone?"

Mr. Graber shrugged. "Sometimes there is anger mixed with other feelings. Maybe you're confused because you feel bad for being angry that he left."

"I don't feel mad at him. How is that?" She didn't know why her question came out so sharply. Was it true? Had she been angry with Daniel?

Shrugging again, the old man took another bite of the apple and chewed slowly before responding. "You were left. You said yourself that others now gossip about you. Talk about you and treat you differently. Anger only makes sense."

His eyes bored into her and Mercy found herself admitting it, as she stared at the empty plate on her lap, "Perhaps. I should pray for him, shouldn't I? Worry about him living in the *Englischer* world, away from a plain, Godly life? But it shouldn't be that my greatest loss is…not having the life I expected. Not being a *Frau*."

Graber threw the remaining apple core across a fence that separated the yard from a field. "I don't know if you ever loved him, but I know about being left."

That brought her head up to stare at him. "*Yah*. Yet your *Frau* died. She did not choose to walk away. Perhaps I didn't love Daniel the way you loved your wife."

"Maybe not. But we're still in the same situation, you and I. My *Frau* left me. I am alone." He fell silent, gazing ahead at the busy farm yard with no expression.

107

As strange as it was to be sitting here, talking so intimately with this grieving, angry *Mann*, Mercy felt oddly comfortable.

"Maybe by...leaving you, this Daniel did you a service. Maybe *Gott* was working on his heart to make him do what he did before you two married. You may find even greater love." Zacharius shrugged.

"That certainly hadn't occurred to me." Mercy sat in silence for a few moments before blurting out, "Isaac Miller wants to...to court me. But an *Englischer* is trying to get Isaac to leave the church and move to work for him.

She ducked her head. "I...I like Isaac. Maybe more than like him, but how can I accept in him what I wouldn't even consider accepting with Daniel?"

Zacharius looked at her steadily, the chatter of the other church members filtering over to them.

"Maybe this Isaac has hold of your heart as Daniel never did."

Mercy looked down at the patch of grass she'd been plucking. "I haven't known him, but a short time."

"*Neh*. It happens that way sometimes. I had known my Ada all our lives...but we didn't really see one another until after her first husband died. Then when we did, it wasn't any time at all before I loved her. Maybe it was this fast with you and Isaac Miller."

"Maybe...although I still don't feel...right about it. After Daniel." She saw several families starting to gather young children then, as in preparation to leave.

"So what do you think I should do?" She reached for his used plate.

"*Maedel*," he recommended, "listen to your heart. It's good you didn't marry if you didn't love. I may not have found my *Frau* until later in life and she may have left me too soon, but I loved that woman. And she loved me better than any other could. You should have the same."

"*Aaeeeiii!*" As the dodge ball bounced off the side of her head, Mercy's shriek echoed in the little hollow in front of the Schneider home.

"Sorry!" called out one of the opposing team's *Menner*. "I didn't mean to throw it yet."

Isaac dove after the mistakenly thrown ball, shifting towards Mercy to call out to her as he tossed it back to the young Mann, "Are you alright?"

"Sure." She sent him an unsmiling look as she straightened her black *Kapp*, pulling out the bobby pins to refasten it. "I like being surprised by a dodge ball in the face."

As the afternoon had progressed, the families with young children had trickled away, the younger members of the community started a game of dodge ball before starting the Sing that was to follow.

Moving back several feet after sending the mistakenly-thrown ball—although he didn't return to his original spot on the dodge ball court—Isaac registered that everything felt different now that he truly wanted to court Mercy. With her warmth and intelligence and beauty, she'd wormed her way into his head before he'd realized it.

At the same time, he felt amused at himself. He was so aware of her, having watched her conversation earlier with old man Graber. The two had talked for a surprisingly long time earlier, off under the shade of that big oak tree. It was startling that Zacharius had conversed with her.

The Sing's host, Mr. Schneider, stood now off to the side. "Are you all ready? Those on this side get the throw first. You have the volley balls? *Gut*. Now when I give the word, start throwing. I'll call out when time is up and we'll see who is left on which side. Okay? Go!"

Isaac dodged and lunged—even dropping to his knees once—in the melee that followed, balls hurtling passed him, catching some of their team members unaware and while others were gathered to be thrown back. As he watched, the play shifted to the other side of the court. The several *Menner* on the other team, jumping forward to return the balls, nailing two players with one throw. Shrieks and cheers came from all sides.

As if he still somehow had a heightened awareness of Mercy, even while jumping to dodge incoming balls and hurtle them back, Isaac could hear her laughter ring out every now and then from a group of girls off to his side. Isaac shifted to one side as a ball flew by him, laughing as he sprang away. Then almost as in slow motion, he saw a ball sailing toward Mercy—and he jumped toward her.

To his own surprise—to say nothing of hers—he shoved Mercy down hard, pushing her out of the path of the incoming missile.

One moment, she stood facing the other team and the next, she was stretched out on the ground.

Isaac dodged side-to-side to avoid the balls, both as their team members threw them and as they were returned by the opposite team, making his way to where Mercy had fallen, appearing to try to recover.

"Are you okay?" he panted.

She looked up at him stonily. "Stop asking me that, Isaac."

Mercy sat beside Isaac three hours later, the night covering them as the buggy horse made his way down the road. "You didn't have to take me home. I could have gotten a ride from the one of the other girls at the Sing."

She knew her voice was cool, even though she'd allowed him to sit next to her at the Singing and to bring her a plate of goodies later.

"Are you still mad at me?"

In the dim light, she saw his broad hat swivel toward her. He insisted again, "I said I was sorry."

A scoffing sound slipped out of her. "Oh, he's sorry he shoved me to the ground so he could return the ball. Tell that to my bruised…parts."

There was no denying, though, that she always had fun with Isaac—dripping wet with a sprained ankle or flat on her bruised behind in a dodge ball game.

"Being with you is clearly dangerous to my continued health," she offered even as the thought pinged in her head that she'd never had this much fun with Daniel. Ever. The realization again stirred feelings of guilt in her and made her feel she should...she didn't know, consider Daniel's newest plea? No! She didn't want to live in the *Englischer* world.

Isaac dropped the reins, reaching over to clasp her hands, jerking her out of her pointless musing.

The cool dark of the night was filled with the sound of insects and creeping things. A feathery breeze whispered past.

"I never wanted to bruise any part of you." Isaac's words were said in a low, sincere voice. "Do you know why I pushed you, Mercy? I've been thinking about it. This kind of thing isn't like me. Lots of girls have played on dodge ball teams with me before, but I've never gone so far to try and protect one."

"So you didn't knock me down because you just had to throw that ball back," she responded promptly, allowing her hands to remain clasped by his larger, warm ones.

"*Neh*, it had nothing to do with returning the ball."

Sitting close on the buggy seat, his hands holding hers, shouldn't have had this effect on her, Mercy knew. But this was Isaac, the *Mann* who teased and tempted her... The one who'd agreed to help her fend off *Aenti* and *Onkle's* determined, relentless matchmaking. The *Mann* who claimed to want to court her battered princess self for real.

Mercy's heart speeded up, the low vibration of his warm, earnest voice mingling with the hum she felt every time he touched her. But tingling didn't mean she felt the same for him as Zacharius felt for his *Frau*.

She needed to remember that. Isaac tended to make her forget...pretty much everything.

"This is why I shoved you down," he said drawing her closer. "This is why I had to keep that ball from hitting you."

Then he kissed her and all the heat between them exploded in her head as his mouth moved gently against hers. It was as the times before when they kissed, only more. And better.

When finally Isaac lifted his head, he drew a deep breath. "I saw that ball flying toward you…and I had to protect you…by shoving you."

His chuckles filled the air and she felt the arms around her shaking with his laughter. Knowing she, too, was grinning at the irony of what he said, she pushed a little against his chest. "So maybe we shouldn't be on the same team next time. We can compete against each another—like at the last Sing—and you'll try to bean me with the ball because you want to win. Maybe you won't have this strange urge to knock me down."

Isaac laughed more, squeezing her in his arms before his mirth died away. He bent to kiss her again and she clung to his shoulders, breathless when he ended it. "Speaking of teams, I think maybe—" he was breathing hard, as well—"you and I should be one. A team, I mean."

Mercy gulped in another breath.

"Court with me, Mercy," his amusement vibrated in his urging words, "and I promise never to again shove you down in dodge ball."

"That's a reason to court," she teased. It was still hard to believe he truly meant it, that he wasn't just caught up in their pretense. That he, too, wouldn't leave. Yet she found herself powerfully drawn to him in a way she'd never felt for Daniel. If only *Gott* would speak to her and give her divine direction.

"It is a tempting idea, Isaac," she continued, returned with a smile. "I might just take you up on that offer. Maybe."

CHAPTER EIGHT

Several days later, Isaac stood in front of his fragrant wood shop, frowning as he brushed the sawdust from his hands. "What do you mean, Mr. Abbott?"

The *Englischer* smiled. "It's very simple, Isaac. As I said, I'm offering you a job, but more than that. I want to feature your furniture in a special, new line. Your furniture is simple and elegant. Piece after piece."

"Thank you for the compliment." Behind his house the morning sun shone warm on Isaac's head. "I'm glad the pieces you bought worked well for you, but as you see, I have a farm here. I told you before I don't need a job."

"Listen, Isaac." The dark-haired *Englischer* shifted, his expression sharpening. "Let me explain. I may not have been clear before. This is too great an opportunity to miss. I want to start a whole line featuring your furniture. You are to design each piece yourself, choose and train each furniture maker and watch production to ensure quality of every item. Give each piece close and personal attention to make sure they're all up to our high standards. I think it will be a big seller and make a lot of money."

Isaac stared at him, trying to comprehend what the man was saying. "You want to buy everything I make?"

Abbott leaned forward, his gaze locked on Isaac's as an excited smile broadened the man's expression. "No, Isaac. Not just the things you make here in your little workshop. I want to start an entire line from my furniture factory. We have a production capacity ten times what you could do here."

Slowly straightening from the spot where he'd been leaning against his work bench, Isaac said slowly. "Leave this place? To work for you in another town?"

"Yes. I'll pay you a significant salary. You'll work for me." Mr. Abbott then named a salary that made Isaac blink.

While he was a rascal in many ways, Isaac's *Daed*, Samuel, had taught all his sons to be hard-headed about money. And this was more money than Isaac had ever seen.

He had a sudden, overwhelming desire for *Gott* to give him direction.

Slowly Isaac said, "Let me...think about your proposition, Mr. Abbott."

"Mr. Graber!" Mercy saw the old man sitting grey-faced on a log by the bridge nearly a week after their conversation after the worship service.

"*Goedenmorgan, Maedel*." Zacharius Graber sounded better than he'd looked at first glance. "Headed to Bontreger's?"

As the store was just ahead, this wasn't a surprising guess. "*Aenti* needs a few things for the kitchen. Are you alright?"

"Of course." He sounded as irritable as usual. "I'm just resting here. Can't a *Mann* rest without all these questions?"

Mercy seated herself on the log next to him, gathering her long skirt around her ankles. She said calmly, "You know you don't have to answer my questions. You've certainly ignored me before."

Their conversation under the tree at the Schneider's earlier in the week made her more comfortable with him. She really had no doubts about what she'd said to Daniel, but she felt better for having talked about it. Her secret was safe with the elderly *Mann*. Zacharius Graber certainly wouldn't gab about it to anyone. Surveying him from her position next to him, she dared to ask, "Is your weariness not abating?"

He cast her a sharp look of dislike. "*Neh*, and before you ask, I've not tried that nasty tea you gave me."

"Why not? You cannot know the tea will taste nasty if you've not tried it."

"All potions taste nasty."

He sounded like a fretful child and she found herself smiling. "This is a tea, not a potion. I've not added anything to it, certainly nothing to make it taste bad."

He looked down at the bare dirt in front where they sat on the log, using a stick to poke at the ground. "I don't cook much."

"Why not?" she asked in an even voice. "You must eat."

"Cooking doesn't seem worth the effort when there's just one person." He scratched more at the dirt in front of them.

"Mr. Graber do you not have any relatives around here?" She'd often wondered how he could be so alone. "Do you not have brothers and sisters?"

"I did," he responded in a less ruffled tone. "But they've moved away years ago to farms of their own—or they died. The three oldest have gone to be with *Gott*."

There was something about the way he said it that made her look at him sharply. "Are you wishing, Mr. Graber, that you, too, might go to be with *Gott*?"

He didn't say anything to this and she felt impelled to say, "For many, it is hard to go on…when they've lost special people like your wife."

Zacharius just stared at the dirt he was gouging with the stick.

She knit her hands together, saying quietly, "When my *Grossmammi* died, I was very sad for a long time. We were very close and spent a lot of time together. I cried and cried, but my *Mamm* and *Daed* reminded me that life was given of *Gott* and that we all had to go on living—worshipping *Gott* and being a reflection to others. They also pointed out that my *Grossmammi* would want this of me."

Silence fell between them, but Mercy thought it was a companionable moment. "I loved my *Grossmammi* so much. It was she that taught me about beneficial herbs and all the plants *Gott* gave us for healing."

After a moment, Zacharius said in a rusty voice, "She must have been a fine woman."

"She was." Sitting quietly beside him, Mercy knew pushing him wouldn't help. This sorting through of challenging events— well, she understood from her own struggle that each had a right to wrestle in their own time. Her *Onkle* and *Aenti* didn't seem to have any concept of the reality.

Finally old man Graber seemed to draw himself from whatever thoughts he'd been contemplating. "It was your *Grossmammi* that told you about the tea you gave me?"

"*Yah.*"

Zacharius cleared his throat. "Well, maybe I'll make the tea then. It—it can't hurt me and—maybe I'll be less tired."

Reaching out, Mercy put her hand over his, stopping his poking in the dirt. "I have been praying that you might do this and feel better."

Their gazed locked, his hand still under hers, Graber let a brief smile crease his face. "I'll try the tea, *Maedel*, but what will make you feel better? Have you decided about this new courtship? Might this Isaac be the *Mann* for you?"

"*der Vedder?*" Isaac sat next to his father as Samuel's buggy rumbled down the road a week later. "*Denki* for taking me to spend time with Mercy."

His father glanced over with a smile. "Of course."

"I finished my work in the fields early today and am able to spare the time." He knew he'd mentioned the farm because Samuel and Enoch sometimes accused him of neglecting his crops to spend time in the workshop.

"I'm just glad you came by my *Haus* for a visit. Taking you to see Mercy—" his father sent him a teasing glance, "who you are only pretending to court—is no problem at all since I'm driving over to Enoch's to get the mulch. Besides, I like Mercy."

Feeling a sheepish smile widen his mouth, Isaac admitted, "I'm not just pretending anymore."

His *Daed* patted his knee. "I know, *der Suh*. I know."

The *Englischer's* proposition had still been playing around in Isaac's head. While he'd seen no reason to speak to anyone else about it, he now felt the tug of impulse to tell Samuel.

"Something interesting happened with that *Englischer Mann* I've sold to at the roadside farm stand the other day," Isaac said after deliberating. "He came by my farm to speak to me."

"*Yah?*" His *Daed* looked over, waiting for him to finish.

"*Yah.* That *Englischer* who has been buying different things from me..." Isaac's mouth felt dry and his hands resting on his knees suddenly felt huge. He had no idea why it was so hard to talk about this. It wasn't as if he'd agreed to this invitation. "Well, he offered me a job."

"He did? But surely he knows you have a farm?" Samuel clucked to get the buggy horse moving through a turn. "Your *Mamm* and I made sure to save the money for all you boys to have farms. When a *Mann* has a farm, he doesn't need another job."

Recognizing that he hadn't conveyed the offer completely, Isaac tried again. "It wasn't just a job, *Daed*. He wants me to design an entire bunch of furniture for him. A furniture line, he called it. He talked of wanting me to hire and train workers...and of wanting me to move to the city to do all this."

"Oh." As the buggy trotted up a bigger road, Samuel said nothing else, just cast a waiting glance at his son.

"I told him I needed to think about it, but I'm leaning toward saying no. I have become a member of the church." Isaac knew Mercy was accurate in talking of Amish parents fearing that their children would leave the simple, plain Godly life for the gaudy, sinful *Englischer* world. "I like building things, but I-I cannot see living that life. Even though, it is so much money."

Samuel didn't immediately say anything to this, just guided the buggy along the road, but Isaac heard his father's relieved release of breath.

"There is no way to do this, what the *Englischer* asks, is there *der Vedder*?" Isaac stared through the buggy windscreen. "I do have the farm to look after and that takes most of my time. It's just that you've always spoken to us about being…provident. Mindful of our money. Also about working to see *Gott's* direction. What do you think I should do? Do you agree that I should do as seems clear to me and tell him no?"

"It is important to work always to hear *Gott's* voice," Samuel said finally, "and I cannot see him leading you away from our life here. Despite the money. I do agree with your decision."

Isaac had initially had the same response to Mr. Abbott's offer, but still, it was a hard possibility to completely dismiss.

"Have you spoken to Mercy about this?"

As though stung, Isaac swung around to look at his father. "*Neh*! No, I have not. Why do you ask?"

Samuel clucked at the buggy horse again. "Well, *der Suh*, your mother would have had my hide if I tried to keep her out of a decision like this."

"Are you sure my son isn't in your way?" Samuel smiled at Mercy from the fence surrounding her *Aenti's* garden patch a few minutes later. "Isn't the meeting here tomorrow? Bishop Yoder and his *Frau* may be too busy for visitors."

"Thanks, *Daed*," was Isaac's dry response to this. Looking down at Mercy, squatted on the dirt with her work dress skirt billowing around her and the black of her *Kapp* already begrimed with dirt from the garden, he felt his heart swell. She was a kind, loving woman and he felt more drawn to her every day. Even if he hadn't been immediately sure of how to handle Mr. Abbott's offer, Isaac knew he fit with Mercy.

Mercy who'd already said she wouldn't leave this life.

Isaac hadn't confessed to anyone his role in Daniel's departure. He kept telling himself that it was between only *Gott* and him, but the shadow of Daniel and his abandonment of Mercy—along with his plain life—still hung between her and Isaac. He felt it, but he couldn't find a way to confess this to her without losing any chance with her.

Mercy smiled from her spot on ground, responding to his *Daed's* question. "*Yah*, the meeting is here and I'm sure *Onkle* and *Aenti* will put Isaac to work, if they need help preparing the *Haus*."

From his spot next to his *Daed* as they leaned over the fence, Isaac lifted his brows sardonically. "Oh, joy. Are you sure you don't need me in the garden?"

Samuel chuckled as Mercy grinned up at his son.

She sent him a twinkling smile. "Don't you want to give my *Onkle* and *Aenti* a reason to like you better? It could make life more pleasant."

"Well, I do want life to be more pleasant." Isaac walked around to the gate into her garden plot. "If they desire, I'll gladly help prepare the *Haus*."

"Well," Samuel straightened, "I must get some mulch from Enoch. He bought extra for us all since it was cheaper that way. I usually make my own, but more is always better."

"You go on." Isaac smiled at his father. "I'll walk home. Thanks for the ride here."

After his father had driven his buggy down the drive, Isaac squatted next to Mercy. "Your *Aenti* and *Onkle* aren't around now? Can I steal a kiss?"

She straightened to her feet, bare in the freshly-turned garden furrow, holding out a garden fork. "*Neh, Schavuit.* But you can clean that spot over there in the garden and turn the dirt so I can plant again."

"Slave driver," he muttered with playful disappointment, receiving the garden fork into his hand. He did want to kiss her, but he didn't want her distracted by worry that her *Onkle* would walk around the corner of the *Haus*. "Here I thought this was going to be fun."

119

She lifted a brow as she continued holding out the gardening impliment, although she smiled without saying anything.

He took it and started loosening the piece of ground she'd indicated, reflecting that if he'd taken Mr. Abbott's offer, it would have meant abandoning all hope of more afternoons like this with Mercy. She'd made it very clear that she didn't want another kind of life. Not to mention that it would mean leaving this home he loved...even if he did find the money part of Mr. Abbott's proposition interesting. Isaac didn't think he could be happy away from Mercy or his life here.

Grinning at her as he lifted the fork and stuck it in again. "Doing this with you, however, is more fun than working in my own fields or in my workshop. I don't suppose you're looking for work in either one of these jobs?"

"No, I'm not. You are so silly, Isaac." Mercy shifted forward to yank at several weeds.

"Tell me about your days back home," he said, shoving aside his thoughts about spending all his time building things, as he would if he'd taken the *Englischer's* offer. He'd have missed planting and growing crops. "You must have had a garden. Do you find many herbs growing in the fields there?"

Mercy sent him a surprised look. "You don't really care about herbs."

She said it with tolerant amusement, but he protested anyway, "*Yah*, I do. At least, I want to learn more about you and I know you've developed quite a knowledge of herbal health uses. This is why I was taking you across the stream to the special fields where herbs grow. I don't particularly care about herbs, but I...care about your interests."

Mercy sat down on the dirt near the fence, bending forward to carefully tease out some of the green plants growing there in a row. "The mysterious 'special field' of herbs across the stream. I remember. In answer to your question, *Yah*. I do have a garden— well, a corner of our produce garden. And there are some herbs I gather from the fields."

Watching her thin out the green row with such brow-furrowing concentration made him want to throw himself down next to her and draw Mercy into his arms. He didn't, of course.

The warm sun shone strong on them and Isaac was glad he'd kept on his wide-brimmed straw hat to throw some shade on his face. "Do friends and family often ask you to recommend healing tonics? Do they ask you to make them concoctions?"

"*Yah*, some do. I worked with my *Grossmammi* as a *Maedel*," she responded finally. "Friends came from all over to get her help. It was better than paying more for an *Englischer* doctor and very often better for them."

She scooted along the row of plants to a new section.

Isaac kept digging in the square area of the garden, pulling out stalks of spent plants and loosening the dirt. "And because you worked with your *Grossmammi*, the community knew that you have her recipes?"

Mercy nodded. "Helping in that way—using the plants *Gott* gave us—made me feel closer to her and useful in an important way."

Isaac stepped down to push the garden fork into the earth. "Well, your knowledge certainly helped *Boppli* Elizabeth…and the whole family. Enoch wasn't much fun without sleep."

She laughed. "Probably not. I love my garden patch at home—my *Mamm* is tending it—and of course I help with the animals around the farm." She scratched at her chin with a dirty hand, leaving a smudge there.

"And friends?" He grinned at her. "You are such a lively, fun woman, I know you must have friends there."

Mercy blushed, shoving the back of her grimy hand along her chin. "*Denki*. I used to think I had friends. More friends, anyway. *Maedels* I'd grown up with. We had such fun together then, quilting and putting up preserves with our *Mamms*. Sewing dresses. You know, doing girl things. We went to Sings with the boys and I even won a horse race once."

"You're better at that than at dodge ball?" he ventured audaciously.

"*Yah*." She made a face at him. "But don't worry. From now on, I know how dodge ball is played here and I'll look out for players who shove their team mates to the ground."

He laughed, then said quietly, "So, what happened with your friends when Daniel left? Why did they not stand by you?"

Mercy picked up a nearby trowel and began loosening the soil at the base of the plants. "They did, at first. Several of them, anyway. But you must see that no one could understand why he'd left so suddenly. It wasn't as if he'd talked to them about having questions. They didn't understand any more than I did."

"Daniel…" she shook her head, "he wasn't that way. Not clearly restless and challenging the rules. Looking back, I can see that he…never seemed to know quite what he should do. But without knowing why he left, some people even questioned whether I'd done something really bad to make him leave."

Isaac stopped digging, his foot on the fork. "What do you mean? How could you make Daniel leave? I mean, I can't think of any reason marrying you might trigger that, other than him not being able to face being a husband and father."

He went back to pushing the garden tool into the dirt. "It sounds like his problem more than yours."

She didn't say anything to this, just continuing to work her way along the garden rows, looking beautiful and smudged with soil.

The way wisps of her blond hair at her neck escaped her grimy *Kapp*, glistening damp in the sun, made Isaac want to press his mouth there. He didn't of course. She hadn't yet agreed to actually court with him, even if she had returned his kisses.

"*Denki*, for saying that, Isaac," Mercy said finally, looking up at where he was still loosening the soil.

Confused, he said, "For what?"

She went back to thinning out the row. "For believing it wasn't my fault that Daniel left."

He knew he should have said it then. Should have just blurted out that he knew it wasn't her fault because the blame was his. He didn't, though. To his shame, Isaac's mouth felt glued shut.

Unable to force out the words he feared would part her from him forever, he just nodded and sent her a smile that felt as weak as he knew himself to be.

"Why did you not leave with him?" The question was out of his mouth before Isaac realized it. "I mean, the only thing you said once was that you didn't want to leave this life… But you and he had courted. Didn't you have…thoughts of going with him?"

She stopped pulling out seedlings. "I—I must be honest with myself, don't I? Surely I would have had those thoughts if I truly loved him, wouldn't I? I guess I realized when he left—without him asking me to go with him—that I wouldn't have left with him anyway because I didn't love him. Not like that. Not really."

His foot still resting motionless on the garden fork, Isaac regarded her, the consciousness of his own guilt lightening a little.

"If I ever court with a *Mann* again," she said suddenly, "I will love him. Truly. So that the biggest part of his leaving will make a hole in my heart. Like Zacharius Graber when his *Frau* died."

More than anything in that moment, Isaac wanted to be loved like that. "Mercy, I also cannot see leaving this life."

"*Neh?*" She lifted her head to look at him, puzzlement in her blue eyes.

He stepped on the back of the garden fork to push it into the dirt.

Isaac had blurted the words out, not having planned to say anything, but compelled. "I was recently offered an *Englischer* job—one that paid a lot of money—by an *Englischer* who wants me to move to the city and design furniture for him."

Mercy's face seemed to pale as she looked up at him. "You were?"

"*Yah.*" Isaac lifted the fork, shaking the dirt from it. "But after considering the offer carefully, I'm going to tell him no."

He smiled at her, saying deliberately. "I don't want to leave this life either or…the people here. I especially don't want to leave you."

Isaac clucked to his big farm horses as they started down the next row with the plow. Behind him, half the fallow pasture had been ploughed into furrows ready for planting, the rich dark soil ready for his fall crops.

But his mind wasn't on the work. Mechanical in the accustomed rhythm of walking behind the large, muscular horses, he held the plow upright as they dragged it forward, the sharp blade cleaving through the weed grass.

Thoughts flashed through his head—Mercy admonishing him all those weeks ago to let her speak to distraught little Sarah at Bontreger's store. Mercy standing in the stream at his encouragement, her face wrinkled in the pain of her wrenched ankle.

She hadn't blamed him for that, even letting him hoist her on his back to carry her out of the water. Not that she'd had a lot of choice, but still, she hadn't angrily refused to speak with him as other girls might have done. He couldn't live without her beside him. Somehow he had to get her to agree to their courtship.

A remembrance of the two of them sitting on the bank drying off afterwards made him smile as he automatically stopped the horses at the end of the row, waiting as they shifted around.

Even more since working with her in the Yoder's garden, he'd had thoughts of her running through his mind.

He loved her. That was part of the reason he'd decided to tell Mr. Abbott no, his love for Mercy and the confirmation in his own mind that he wanted to remain here on his farm…with her. Talking with his *Daed* had helped. Isaac felt with Mercy as he couldn't have imagined feeling with any other woman. In that moment, he wanted more than anything to be the *Mann* she loved like Zacharius had loved his *Frau*.

Continuing to follow the plow, the realization of his love for Mercy collided with a completely an unusual sense of doubt. Did she like him as much as he liked her? Perhaps that was why she hadn't agreed to court with him. Did she still love Daniel somewhere down deep, despite having claimed not to?

If not, could she love Isaac? Of course, he'd doubted himself in many ways before, but he'd always flirted easily with girls. Always walked away freely if one didn't respond. In that moment, he wasn't sure he'd be able to recover if Mercy didn't return his love.

CHAPTER NINE

After the church meeting several days later, Enoch dove toward his little blonde daughter who'd been toddling toward the fire place, stopping when Isaac reached her first.

Halted in her own leap from the Yoder kitchen toward the child, Mercy watched Isaac snatch up Kate and Enoch's little girl. "Whoa! Little *Boppli* Lizzie!" He nuzzled her pink cheek. "We don't want you cooked!"

Behind them the fireplace simmered even though the day was warm.

Tossed above Isaac's head, the *Boppli* shrieked with joy, her infectious gurgle breaking out.

"Isn't she getting to be a big girl?" Kate asked fondly, coming up to rest her hand on Mercy's shoulder. "Enoch and Sarah spoil her terribly. Isaac and her *Grossdaddi* Samuel are no better."

She glanced at Mercy—still watching the two—saying deliberately. "Isaac needs *Bopplis* of his own. He'll make a wonderful father. So playful."

"Elizabeth is getting big and she's walking so well now!" Not ready to commit herself even to Kate, Mercy agreed with her friend's first comment, turning back to the warm, crowded kitchen. The smell of yummy cooking food filled the *Haus*.

"*Yah*, she is walking well," Kate agreed with a twinkling smile that said she recognized the ploy.

Scurrying around to feed the group now that the meeting had ended, the women gathered around her *Aenti* at the stove. White

Kapp askew as she fluttered around the warm kitchen, *Aenti* seemed quite frazzled as she tried to pull the meal together.

As they entered the kitchen area Kate nudged Mercy with an elbow, a teasing smile on her face. "You didn't answer. Don't you think Isaac will make a wonderful father?"

"You need to stop meddling," Mercy said with mock severity as the warmth from the wood stove enveloped them. "Don't you know better?"

Laughing, Kate said "*Neh*," before turning to join the crowd around the stove, calm as she entered into an activity at which she excelled.

Involuntarily glancing back at Isaac, Mercy saw that he'd now tucked the bundle that was little Elizabeth into the crook of his arm and was adjusting the *Boppli* in his hold to let her achieve her goal of stuffing her shoe into her mouth. Enoch stood near them to the side of the mantel with his older *Dochder*, Sarah, tugging at his hand as he leaned over to catch some comment made to him by an elderly *Mann* in a chair beside the fireplace.

Clearly, Enoch was very comfortable leaving his precious *Boppli* in Isaac's care.

As if making nothing of having the responsibility for his *Bruder's* infant child, Isaac stood talking to several of his friends, still cradling the toddler. He hadn't handed the child off to the closest *Frau* as soon as he could. He just...assumed care of the *Boppli*.

The realization hit Mercy all of a sudden, striking to her core, and she paused in her kitchen job, staring. The *Menner* she knew usually left their children to their wives' care. Isaac's easy attention to his little niece was startling and it made her chest tighten in a strange way.

She'd laughed and teased with him—thought about whether she should allow him to truly court her—and been relieved that he hadn't let the furniture *Englischer* tempt him away. But...now with a realization that seemed blinding, she saw him as way more than the *Schaviut* she always teased him about being.

She loved him. She loved Isaac.

127

The brisk, noisy bustle around Mercy quickly called her attention back to her job at hand and she went on ladling cooked vegetables into several big bowls, trying to act normal even though she'd just been struck through with her realization.

As usual, the chatty congregation was hungry and eagerly took their spots at the tables as the younger women moved around, putting bowls of food out and replacing these as soon as the rotating lunch crowd emptied them. As she slipped between the tables to place bowls of mashed potatoes Mercy thought that she felt more comfortable in this group, even than in the town where she'd grown up. Of course that might be different with some time having passed since Daniel left, but still.

After settling the last of her bowls on the table, she put up a hand to make sure her *Kapp* hadn't come loose from its pins, heading back to the kitchen area.

Both nothing and so much had changed since Daniel had gone away…and now he'd popped up, inviting her to leave her home to join the world he'd chosen. She could never do that. Leaving her life, her family and the friends she'd made here was impossible…as was the thought of leaving Isaac. This was manner of worship she practiced, but Daniel didn't recognize it.

She'd not liked the pitiful look of him. As she moved between the tables—going back and forth to the kitchen for refills—she arranged a pleasant smile on her face, but she found herself wishing and hoping that Daniel would never again return. She couldn't hope harm for him, even if *Gott* would not forbid that, but she didn't want to shun Daniel. She already had guilt over her realization that she'd never truly loved him as she should have.

Not as she loved Isaac.

Passing out the food, she saw Isaac sitting at one of the tables with several other young *Menner* and on his knee sat *Boppli* Elizabeth. Mercy moved through the maze of tables, her ears tuned on the laughing conversation among the group. Their conversation bounced between subjects and all the while, Isaac provided the *Boppli* with tidbits. Turning with a stack of crockery in her hands, she saw the child chewing on a crust of roll, her insides growing warm and mushy at the sight of him with the Boppli.

Kate was right. He'd be a wonderful *Daed*.

Starting to collect more used dishes after the last of the church members gradually drifted away from them, Mercy trekked back and forth to the sink where several others were washing.

Finding her gaze again straying to Isaac, she noted he was leaving the *Haus*, *Boppli* still in his arms. With her rosy cheeks and her tiny black *Kapp*, she was cute as a button, her chubby hand clutching Isaac's jacket.

Later that afternoon, Mercy escaped the warmth of the kitchen when all was clean, going out to the porch.

Sitting in chairs there were several older *Fraus* and Mercy was aware that they stopped talking when she came out of the *Haus*. One woman was saying "...and they had courted and were to be married—"

Another *Frau* in the group then hissed at her just as the screen door closed behind Mercy when she came out onto the porch. It wasn't the first time something like this had happened and as was her habit these days, she smiled at them before descending the steps, ignoring what she'd overheard.

With a sigh, as she went down the stairs, Mercy reminded herself that there was no point in making any comment. A quick glance told her that among the group of women sat *Frau* Fisher whose sister lived in the same town where Mercy and Daniel had grown up and who had a son just about Daniel's age.

Even though she'd gotten more comfortable here, she knew Daniel's desertion followed her. She hadn't gone to the *Englischer* world with him, but she still represented the fears of many *Eldre*.

Crossing the farm house yard, she passed several clusters of people she knew, cheered by their calling out to thank her for the lunch she'd helped serve. Responding to Kate's beckoning, Mercy found her friend under a tree with Samuel, Enoch and Sarah. They stood near a pen of fencing attached to the big barn.

"Mercy!"

She saw that Hannah, her husband, John, and their eldest daughter stood there with Kate's family and all were looking at something in the pen by the barn.

"You can see that the *Liebling* is a natural." Hannah chuckled, her arm around her elder daughter.

As she drew closer, Mercy realized Isaac trotted on a horse inside the pen, little Elizabeth held on the saddle in front of him.

"Is she not fearless?" Enoch beamed at the *Boppli*, hoisting Sarah onto his shoulders, despite the fact that she wasn't a small fry anymore. "Look, Sarah. You'll have to teach Lizzie to drive the buggy soon."

Reaching where they stood as the group all broke out in laughter at his prediction, Mercy stopped next to her friend, staring into the pen at Isaac and the *Boppli* with that same constricted feeling in her chest as she'd had earlier when acknowledging to herself that she loved him. Seeming unaware of his unusual actions, Isaac directed the docile horse in circles around the pen, the laughing child in his hands clutching the horse's mane.

"I have tried to take Elizabeth from him several times," Kate commented with a smile, "but she cried whenever I started to take her from Isaac. I think she's fallen in love with him."

Mercy stood there watching the *Mann* who'd been trying to court her for several weeks. She'd also fallen in love with Isaac.

"I'm so glad you let me take you home." Isaac turned to smile at her as the afternoon sun slanted rich through the tree branches when they rode past.

"I'm glad you asked." Mercy looked down at where she'd plaited her fingers together in her lap.

Staring ahead as she sat on the hard buggy seat next to him, she was flooded again with the thought that Isaac was a *gut* man, that he could be trusted even with darkest secrets. Over and over, he'd proved that—agreeing to participate in the courtship charade to make *Onkle* and *Aenti* back off, carrying her from the stream when she'd sprained her ankle and never once grabbing a part of her that he shouldn't. All these things he'd done without getting anything himself—except maybe taking a small delight in annoying *Onkle* Yoder.

And then today, being so kind and attentive with *Boppli* Elizabeth. She loved him.

"You were so busy with the *Boppli* that we didn't get much of a chance to talk today."

His chuckle was rich. "She's a wonderful little girl and she'll give other kids a run for their money."

The summer evening breeze brought with it the fresh earthy smell of the grass and countryside as the horse trotted down the lane, its harness faintly jingling.

As softened as her heart was to Isaac, it felt wrong to keep from him that she'd spoken to Daniel. Even if she felt shy of telling him the feelings she realized she had for Isaac, she needed to tell him of this. She swallowed and ducked her head before saying, "I want to tell you something, Isaac."

Looking away from the road again, he paused and then said, "Of course. What is it?"

"I know it was wrong and I shouldn't have, but...I-I've spoken to Daniel. Even though he's shunned." The last phrase came out in a rush and her breath suspended tightly in her chest, waiting for his response. The *Ordnung* was very clear on this. "The entire congregation voted to excommunicate Daniel after he left, rejecting all to which he'd been raised. I know this! But how could I ignore him totally?"

"*Yah*." Isaac's response seemed mechanical.

"I know this shunning is to protect the church faithful from 'bad sheep' who might disrupt the unity of the church, but, Isaac, I grew up with Daniel. He looked so terrible and I couldn't just not respond when he showed up and spoke to me."

In the dimming light, she could see Isaac's capable hands on the buggy reins.

"So, you saw him recently? Here?" He turned to give her a flashing glance.

"Yes. Out behind *Onkle* and *Aenti's* house. I was tending to the washing." The tightness in her chest lessened. "It's a relief to talk to you about it, Isaac."

"I'm glad." He'd turned back to guide the horse. "Tell me all about this."

She sighed again in relief. There was no condemnation in his voice. "It's been almost a month ago and he just showed up in the shadow of their barn one afternoon."

"Because he was worried about you? He should be, leaving you…and everything…that way."

"*Neh*, not just that. I mean," she tried to clarify. "He asked me to join him."

The buggy slowed as Isaac turned to look at her fully. "In the *Englischer* world? He wants you to leave your *Mamm* and *Daed* and all your *Bruders*? The life you've chosen in the church. For him?"

"*Yah*." She nodded, reflecting that Isaac's response was very much like her own.

"Even though you've joined *Gott's* church and committed to this life?" Isaac turned back to cluck at the horse to continue down the road. "He asked all that of you?"

"He did." Mercy turned to look at the passing shadows beneath the beech and maple trees along the lane. She was so relieved to admit her actions. "I said I would not. Would not follow him."

"I can see it would have been very hard not to at least speak to him. You haven't had the chance since he jilted you, have you?"

"*Neh*. We've not spoken since he left." She could see from the tilt of his hat brim that Isaac turned to her.

"Then I can understand this wasn't about disobedience as much as shutting that door fully."

Tears prickled behind her eyes at his complete understanding. She reached over, just touching his bicep before withdrawing her hand. "I feared telling anyone that I'd spoken to him, but you— you are a different matter and I should have known you wouldn't condemn me."

He stretched out his firm, broad hand to clasp her hands where they rested in her lap, saying in a deep voice, "*Neh*, I do not condemn you, Mercy. You can tell me anything."

Later that evening, Mercy finally escaped from all the chores her *Aenti* had given her, holding tight her memory of those precious moments in the buggy with Isaac. With the hours spent at the Sunday service and helping with the evening meal, fear of a further request from her *Aenti* sent her scurrying into the woods as the day began to fade.

She needed time alone to think about…everything. After her realization about Isaac and his sweet response to her confession, she needed a period of quiet to herself.

Actually courting with Isaac had never been in her mind initially. Until it was. She sighed, swishing through the long grass. Her feelings for him had been steadily growing, almost without her realizing it. The other boys in her small town—and the other *Menner* here—hadn't tempted her, at all. Since Daniel's defection, courting with any *Mann* had seemed risky and fraught with danger. Of course, she'd known that someday she'd eventually find the one with whom she wanted to settle down, but she'd only had a vague image of that *Mann*. Someone solid and respectable and steady, with an unshakable devotion to his farm and his *Gott*.

Isaac hadn't looked at all like that at first…

After Daniel, she had completely shied away from the subject of marriage, only thinking of having at some time in the future a courtship with a stolid, reliable someone with whom she'd someday build a home and family. When she'd asked him to help her, Isaac seemed so far away from that. Certainly never a *Mann* who could woo her wary heart and sweep her off her feet. She'd been determined to keep a level head and a toughened heart. Until Isaac.

Somewhere along the way, without knowing it was happening, she'd fallen deeply in love with Isaac. He'd said he wanted to court her in truth and she'd held off considering it until now. But there was no denying that when she'd seen him today with *Boppli* Elizabeth…she'd envisioned him as the father he could be. The *Mann* with whom she could build a home and a family. She'd only been lying to herself in thinking he hadn't gotten to her with his steady loyalty and his joyful smile

He'd always been such a teasing, laughing *Schaviut*. Good with his hands and amazing at crafting furniture from wood…but as she'd watched him in the last weeks, heard of his decision to refuse to be tempted into the *Englischer* world, she let herself realize more and more that she'd fallen in love with him.

It seemed unreal and very real all at once.

Mercy pushed through to a clearing in the wooded area, the sunlight here stronger, but still fading. Sitting down on a mossy log, she folded her skirts around her legs, closed her eyes and prayed. She needed to know if this was the direction *Gott* wanted for her. She'd made such a mistake before. Without question, she knew that she couldn't survive losing Isaac as she'd lost Daniel.

It wasn't anything the same.

"I'm sorry, Mr. Abbott," Isaac looked squarely into the *Englischer's* face across the narrow bench at the farm stand booth. "I've given your proposition serious thought and I must decline it."

Beyond the ten-foot wide booth—displaying several chairs and a table along with two different rocking horses and a cradle— blue skies could be seen. Voices from the other farm stand booths sounded as customers made purchases.

Across the bench, an expression of confusion settled on the *Englischer's* face. "But, Isaac, this is a very lucrative offer. I meant what I said that this would be an entire line of furniture. Made totally to your exact specifications. You'd be in charge of all aspects of the designs, of the crafting. I'd handle all the production matters—the sales parts—other than you choosing the workmen. I think you should reconsider this. You have a real gift."

The *Englischer's* shiny sports car sat in the front of the booth, a symbol of all Isaac was rejecting. He'd gladly take his black buggy and old buggy horse any day.

With a dip of the brim of his broad straw hat, Isaac braced his feet more solidly on the booth's gravel floor and nodded. "I thank you for the compliment, but I must hold to my first answer. I cannot and will not leave my farm and my life here."

"Listen, Isaac, you'll be making enough money to pay people to run your farm." Abbott sounded frustrated. "This could be big for all of us. People will pay for solid wood, well-constructed furniture."

"And I'm sure you'll find plenty of workmen who'll make good furniture for you. I must stay here in my home, worshipping *Gott* as I see fit." He smiled at the *Mann*, appreciating that Abbott had seen something worthwhile in his furniture. "I wish you the best."

Now, he could go ask Mercy the question on his heart.

"Mercy…" Isaac nervously pushed his foot against the porch as he set the swing in motion again. This was so important. He felt the need to marry her bursting within him. He wanted to throw caution to the wind and wrap his arms around her as he declared his love. And yet he also hesitated, knowing this was the biggest step he could take in his life. He needed her to say yes.

"*Yah?*" She glanced at him sideways, sitting next to him on the swing.

He could smell the clean, floral scent of her and he focused his gaze on the tip of his shoe to keep from pulling her close and kissing them both senseless. He'd consciously chosen to speak with her here on her *Onkle's* porch because he knew disapproving eyes watched them and he'd be less likely to succumb to that urge.

"Were you going to say something?" Wearing her navy dress, her black *Kapp* pinned to her neat blond head, she was as beautiful as always.

"Mercy," he started again, "I know I told you that I want to court with you for real— "

"Don't you want to anymore?" She spoke quickly, her fair skin seeming to grow more pale.

"*Neh.*" He swallowed and then took a breath before plunging into speech. "I want to marry you, Mercy. As soon as the harvest is in. As soon as can be arranged, I want to marry you. I want very badly to marry you."

His declaration seemed to startle her and she laughed weakly after a moment. "I thought you were trying to tell me you'd thought better of it. That you don't want to really court with me."

"I don't," Isaac said promptly. "I want to marry you, not just consider marrying you. I don't need to see if we fit together. We do fit. I want you to be my *Frau*, Mercy. I want to love you as Zacharius Graber loved his wife."

Whatever he'd thought and hoped she'd say to this Isaac wasn't prepared when she gave him a wavering smile and burst into tears.

He dropped to the porch's wood floor in front of the swing taking her hand in his. "Mercy, Mercy, please don't cry. I don't ever want to make you cry."

She kept crying in gusty sobs, her hand over her eyes.

He slipped back up on the swing, her smaller hand still in his. "If you don't stop crying, your *Onkle* will come out here do something to me that *Gott* wouldn't approve of."

She laughed at that, a smile dawning on her tear-wet face. "I thought you were done with me. That you were trying to tell me that."

Regardless of the window right next to the swing, Isaac took her in his arms. "We work well together, Mercy. When I'm foolish, you straighten me out or set me on the right path. Just the thought of sharing a life with you helped me be absolutely sure what to say to Mr. Abbott about his offer—I knew I couldn't be happy away from this plain and simple life—or away from you."

His arm still around her and the sensation of her soft womanly curves so close, he sent up a fervent prayer that *Gott* would speak to her in his favor.

Mercy wiped her face with a finger that visibly trembled. "Y-You aren't as foolish as you pretend, you know. You act like a *Schaviut*, but you have this amazing talent with wood and a steady life with *Gott*. You have a kind heart, Isaac, or you'd never have agreed to help me in the first place. I don't believe it was all because of you wanting to tease *Onkle*."

"*Neh*. A beautiful woman asked for my help and in such a way!"

It flashed in his mind just then that he'd really messed up in taunting Daniel that way. It hadn't been either steady or Godly, but it had somehow brought Mercy into his life. He couldn't regret that. Struggling to command his voice—gripped in the sway of her, the wonderful feel of being with her, the soft flowery scent coming off her hair, Isaac said, "I love you, Mercy. Will you wed me and make a life with me?"

Drawing in a shaky voice, she swiped once more at her damp cheek and said with a smile, "*Yah*, not-always-a-rascal Isaac. I will. I love you. I love you as Zacharius loved his *Frau*. I love you as I've never loved anyone."

CHAPTER TEN

"What do you mean you're marrying Isaac Miller?!"

Wincing at her *Onkle* Yoder's thunderous tone later that evening, Mercy could only be glad she'd refused Isaac's offer to break the news to her relatives with her.

"He proposed this afternoon and I accepted." Mercy forced herself to meet the older *Mann's* angry gaze. "*Onkle*, I know you cannot understand why I'm marrying Isaac or why Kate chose to marry Enoch rather than accept Aaron's offer—although Aaron seems fine with it."

Drawing himself up, his face stern over his bristling beard, *Onkle* Yoder seemed to bite back angry words.

As he struggled with himself, she leaned forward and said, "*Onkle*, Isaac is a good *Mann*. He's not—not a *Schlang*—like Daniel. He loves me. Isaac even refused an offer of a lot of money to move to work in the *Englischer* world. He worships *Gott*."

She believed every word and his reaction when she'd told Isaac of Daniel's secret visit had only sealed her conviction that this was the *Mann* for her. Isaac hadn't recoiled in horror that she'd spoken to Daniel. If she'd followed the *Ordnung*, she wouldn't have spoken to him at all since he'd been excommunicated. The elders worked hard to bring straying church members to a realization of their sins. Being shunned was the only option after he'd left their beliefs behind. This was why she hadn't mentioned having spoken to him before. Speaking to a shunned individual was forbidden.

But Isaac had understood.

She had no thought of leaving to be with Daniel, even after the years they'd courted, their plans to marry… but despite him having left, they had a history and she'd needed to say goodbye. Now she could walk away from him.

She still felt conflicted about Daniel. Sad. She couldn't help dwell on whether she should have seen some sign of his thoughts of leaving or whether she'd somehow contributed to his leaving.

A smile curved her lips, just remembering Isaac's immediate rejection of the possibility.

The older *Mann* sitting across from her on the Yoder couch still met her gaze with a blustery, angry glare.

"Please, *Onkle*." Mercy put her hand on Hiram Yoder's knee, resting it briefly on his shiny pant leg before withdrawing it back to clasp her other hand in her lap. "I love Isaac. I'm writing tonight to tell my *Eldre* about my engagement. I know they'll be relieved I've fallen in love with a *Mann* of *Gott* and that I will be happy again."

Onkle Yoder drew a slow, deliberate breath before saying, "*Yah*. You should be with a *Mann* of *Gott* and not pine anymore for that *Schlang,* Daniel. But Isaac Miller! I knew you were courting with him, but I'd hoped— I just wonder if you've given thought to the others here. I have introduced you to several."

"Yes, *Onkle*," she hurried to interrupt. "I know you've done as you believed best. I'm also doing that. I—I love Isaac Miller, *Onkle*. He is not a *Schlang*. There is nothing snake-ish about him. He's strong and—and brave. I believe *Gott* put me here to meet him."

"Well, the Miller family is established and Isaac can support you, having a *gut* farm." *Onkle* Yoder seemed to wrestle with himself again. "If you believe you will be happy with a *Mann* many have called a *Schaviut*—a Miller rascal—then I suppose we must abide by that."

Mercy ignored his unflattering reference to her betrothed, stretching forward in her chair to give him a quick hug. "Thank you for everything, *Onkle* Yoder. If you and *Aenti* hadn't invited me here, I'd never have met Isaac."

Her *Onkle* drew another deep breath. "Well, it had seemed like the right time for a visit. We must rely on Gott to manage things now."

"*Daed*," Isaac said heavily, shifting on the hay bale where he sat in his father's barn.

"*Yah, der Suh*?" Samuel looked up from where he sat on the milking stool next to the Guernsey.

Isaac felt an even heavier burden after Mercy told him she'd spoken to Daniel. "I know you and Enoch and Kate are pleased I'm to marry Mercy—"

"We are." His *Daed* nodded with a big smile. "We are."

"Well," feeling himself flush as he looked down at the straw wisps, Isaac cleared his throat before saying, "I love her, *Daed*. I love Mercy a lot."

"*Yah*, I would hope so." His father sent Isaac a smiling sideways glance, still squatting on the stool in front of the heifer.

The shushing of cow's milk in the pail filled the silence that fell between them.

"But I have done her a great wrong, *Daed*." Isaac let the admission fall out of him. He'd heard Mercy's halting admission of breaking the rules of the *Ordnung* and the sense of his own responsibility for her fiancé's actions had grown until it almost choked him. Feeling both wrenched with guilt and relieved to admit it, he repeated, "I've done her great wrong."

Samuel smiled. "By asking her to be your *Frau*? I wouldn't say that, Isaac. I mean there are those who say you're a *Schaviut*, but…really?"

With a token weak smile for his father's witticism, Isaac said, "No, not that. By—by something I said to Daniel Stoltzfus, the *Mann* she was to marry—when Daniel visited here last summer."

Samuel wiped the cow's teats with a damp cloth that had hung over his knee. Standing to shift the stool over to the next waiting heifer, he paused to look at his son. "What did you say to this Daniel last year, *der Suh*?"

As bad as he felt about his words that evening, it felt good to at last own to his foolishness. "It was when he was here visiting his Glick relatives. There were several of the *youngies* and older *Menner* helping in their fields."

"*Yah*? I remembered that you spent some time out at the Glick farm when Abel fell sick."

Isaac drew a deep breath. Like so many of his moments visiting and working with friends, this mess with Daniel had started off with goofing around. Silliness. His *Eldre* had always warned him his foolishness would one day get him into trouble. "The others had shifted to another side one of the field one late afternoon. It was just this Daniel and I working together."

"*Yah*?" Samuel went on with the milking, indicating that he was still listening by the turn of his head toward his son.

Isaac twisted a wisp of straw between his fingers. "That Daniel Stoltzfus was a fool, not that I'm excusing myself, but he was a silly, boastful *Mann*. More *youngie* than he should have been at that age."

His *Daed* glanced over again, waiting for him to continue, saying nothing about how silly in different ways that Isaac had been himself and Isaac was grateful for this.

"He wouldn't have been a good husband to Mercy." The words came out more forcefully than he'd intended.

Samuel again drew the towel from his knee to wipe the cow he'd just finished milking.

"That Daniel was talking—boasting—about what a good provider he'd be. About how his farm made so much money. This is not how *Gott* wants us to speak. But Daniel, he'd been saying things like that all day." Isaac's chest felt tight remembering.

"Some *Menner* are like that, even though we are told to live the plain and simple life."

"And then he started saying that he could out-farm anyone...even the *Englischers* who use tractors and other means..."

Isaac twirled the hay stalk faster. "And I laughed at him."

"You are a laugher."

Looking up at his *Daed*, Isaac swallowed again. "I laughed at him and said there was no way—unsheltered by his family and without the farm his *Daed* had given him— that he could make it in the *Englischer* world. I said that several times."

Finished with the milking, Samuel settled the milking stool on the pegs set in the wall for it. He stood wiping his hands, watching Isaac.

Isaac dropped the piece of hay, glancing up to meet his *Daed's* eyes. "Several times, I told Daniel he couldn't make it in the *Englischer* world. That he wasn't *Mann* enough."

His father draped the damp towel over another peg and leaned back on a barn post in front of Isaac.

"He argued with me, insisting he could farm better than anyone…and I kept laughing. Saying Daniel was *narrish*. I…I wasn't very nice. *Daed*, I pretty much pushed Daniel into the *Englisch* world, just about dared him to go. I teased him so. But I never thought he'd actually do it."

With his now-empty hands hanging off his knees, his forearms resting on his legs, he told his father. "Daniel left the Glick farm the next day and I heard not two weeks later about him having jilted Mercy and left this life for the *Englischer* world."

The silence in the barn was broken only by the sounds of his *Daed's* milk cows chewing their grain.

Finally, Samuel spoke. "Does anyone know of this? Were any of your friends there to hear you? I think you said the two of you were alone?"

"*Neh*, no one else was there. No one else knows."

"Have you spoken to anyone else about it? To Mercy?"

"No, *Daed*," Isaac said heavily. "I think Mercy would hate me if I had told her. She'd turn her back and never speak to me again. It's been hard for her after Daniel left and some have blamed her for his leaving."

"And, even though no one else knows of this, you still feel guilty for not having confessed your actions to her?"

Isaac nodded, after drawing another long breath. He loved Mercy and it ate at him that he was basically lying to her by not telling her the whole story.

"Have you spoken to *Gott* about this?" His father threw him another needle-sharp glance.

"Many times, but I still don't know what I should do."

"*Der Suh*, much can be forgiven if one repents."

"You're saying I should confess all this to her?" Isaac couldn't even imagine how such a confession would work out well.

"I am saying," his *Daed* straightened from the post and came to lay his arm over Isaac's shoulders, "that *Gott* is with us. Even when we can't see the path."

"I knew it!" Kate's words sounded triumphant the next afternoon as she sat in the Yoder living area next to the blackened fireplace. "I knew you and Isaac were perfect for each other!"

"*Yah*! You sparked off each other immediately." Sitting next to her on the couch, Hannah beamed and nodded, the wisps of her blonde curls bobbing.

Flashing a glance toward where her *Aenti* sat snapping peas in the kitchen, Mercy asked in a quiet voice, "What do you mean?"

"Don't act all sly with us," Kate recommended. "We saw you two from the beginning."

Hannah laughed, her corkscrew tendrils springing loose around her neck. "Of course, it isn't openly announced. These things never are,"

"Mercy," her *Aenti* called over in a voice several degrees cooler than usual. "Would you check the roast in the oven while I step out to the garden for a moment?"

"*Yah, Aenti*." She turned in her seat to send a conciliatory smile toward her aunt.

It was *narrish*! So crazy. She'd started pretending to court with Isaac only to get her *Onkle* and *Aenti* to stop matchmaking, never actually thinking to marry him. Not initially.

143

As her *Aenti* went out the back door to the garden, Mercy slewed back around in her seat to face her friends. "How did the two of you find out that Isaac and I are to marry?"

Since marriages weren't commonly announced until right before the autumn events, neighbors and friends usually had to guess when courtships progressed by watching the amount of celebratory things grown in gardens for wedding feasts. There had been no time, however, for *Onkle* and *Aenti* to have planted celery and such, even if Mercy had planned to marry from their house, which of course she wouldn't. Her *Eldre* would be crushed.

Not that that *Onkle* and *Aenti* felt very celebratory when she'd told them last night that she'd accepted Isaac's proposal. Mercy shuddered when she thought of *Onkle* Yoder's flushed, angry face.

They still hadn't accepted that Kate had chosen Isaac's brother Enoch over their son, Aaron.

Kate's smile widened. "Isaac naturally told his father and Enoch—he was so excited you said yes—."

"And Enoch told you," Mercy concluded, several things becoming clear.

"*Yah.*" Hannah beamed and nodded.

"And I—" Kate giggled.

"You, of course, told Hannah." Mercy couldn't help responding with a smile of her own. She'd felt giddy and excited ever since Isaac had dropped to his knees in front of her. Until then, she'd been afraid he didn't love her. She hadn't even acknowledged to herself how afraid she was of that.

It still warmed her heart to think of his commitment to their life. He'd turned down the *Englischer* and a lot of money.

"…and we all live close to one another." Hannah sighed happily. "We're so happy that you won't live so far away now."

"Although I imagine you'll return to Elizabethtown to be married from your *Eldre's* house." Kate beamed. "This will give James and Gideon—Isaac and Enoch's *Bruders*—a reason to visit this winter. They'll want to meet Isaac's bride."

Mercy felt herself turning pink at the thought. She was finally going to be a bride…and Isaac's bride.

"Mercy," her *Onkle* said when she'd opened her bedroom door that evening.

Glad she hadn't changed out of her day dress yet, she said, "Yes?"

"There are visitors below." He frowned, looking both serious and worried. "Visitors for you. It is Bishop Fisher...and Daniel Stoltzfus is with him."

Already startled to hear that the Bishop from her hometown was here to see her—and was there so late in the evening—Mercy paled when she heard her former fiancé's name, her stomach sinking like a stone in still water.

"Daniel? Daniel is here?" The question sprang stupidly out of her mouth and she dropped the hand she'd held to the door.

"*Yah*." Her *Onkle* motioned her forward. "We must go down, Mercy."

She followed the older *Mann* down the narrow staircase, her long skirt gripped in her hand. What if Daniel had told Bishop Fisher that she'd talked to him, even though he was shunned? Panic rioted in Mercy's chest, calmed only by the thought that she knew Isaac would stand by her.

Rounding the corner into the main room, Mercy came to an abrupt halt several feet away from the stalwart bulk of Bishop Fisher and next to him stood Daniel.

The *Mann* she was to have married oh so long ago looked now as he had that day beside the barn. Thinner and with a drawn face, he was dressed in a black suit she recognized, a broad hat clutched in his hands. His hair was long around his ears and he looked at her with beseeching eyes.

It all seemed so strange. Before he'd left for the *Englischer* world, Daniel had always seemed so confident.

"Mercy?"

Nodding her *Kapped* head without responding verbally, she took only a small step into the room, aware of her *Onkle* beside her. Mercy stared at the floor, waiting tensely.

"We are here, Mercy Yoder," Bishop King said portentously, "to tell you that Daniel Stoltzfus has repented his sinful ways. He has spoken with the church elders and has repented, rejoining the church."

She glanced up then, glancing between Bishop King and Daniel, not sure what all this meant. In her experience, once individuals left and were excommunicated by the church, they didn't return.

Standing next to the bulk of Bishop Fisher, Daniel seemed hunched over and smaller despite his height.

"While his re-avowal is still under study by the elders," The bishop looked both powerful and conscious of the responsibility, "Daniel has renounced the *Englischer* world."

Mercy could only continue to stare at the two of them as Daniel bobbed his head in agreement. She thought she could see in his stiff bearing, some faint sense of compassion behind the bishop's officialdom. He was following his Godly duties, but he didn't seem hostile toward her former fiancé.

"I have accompanied him here at his request," Bishop Fisher announced.

Her *Onkle* moved past Mercy, coming to a stop several paces between her and where Daniel stood. "Why are you here? To what purpose has Daniel Stoltzfus requested you accompany him here, Bishop Fisher?"

The other bishop nodded, as if this question was to be expected. "Well, as I have stated, the elders of the church must pray further with Daniel and confer both amongst themselves and with *Gott*."

From next to Bishop Fisher, Daniel flashed Mercy another pleading glance and then looked back to the floor.

Her thoughts scrambling, any impulse to speak was halted when her *Onkle* erupted.

"*Yah*, of course, but I cannot see how this involves us." *Onkle* Yoder gestured to himself and to Mercy.

At this, Bishop Fisher sent a needle sharp look her way. "Is it not true that Mercy was courting with and planned to marry Daniel? It seems to me that this affects her directly."

Her *Onkle* emitted a short derisive sound. "Mercy has suffered much from this Daniel's actions."

"I am aware." Bishop Fisher nodded.

"Are you suggesting she would resume her plans with him as if nothing has happened?" This was said in an affronted tone and her *Onkle* glared at Daniel.

"Nothing is decided about his re-admittance into our life," Bishop Fisher said.

"Still!" *Onkle* Yoder's scorn was clear as he again gestured at Daniel.

Daniel lifted his gaze to look at Mercy as if she were the only rock amid waters that were drowning him.

"You cannot deny that this involves her, however."

She drew a breath, words colliding as they stumbled out her mouth. "But—but, it doesn't! I'm sorry, Daniel, but I am to marry someone else. I just told my *Aenti* and *Onkle* yesterday that I have fallen in love and am going to marry another *Mann*."

Clearly startled at this unexpected news, Daniel seemed bolted into speech. "Marry? Another *Mann*? But...but who?"

Feeling annoyed that this hadn't even occurred to him, Mercy pressed her lips together, consciously ironing any expression of anger from her face. "I am in love with Isaac Miller."

CHAPTER ELEVEN

Later that night, Mercy knelt by her narrow bed in her room under the eaves at *Onkle* and *Aenti's Haus*, whispering quietly, "Dear *Gott*, What do I do? Am I to…do anything? I betrothed now to Isaac. I love Isaac."

Her plea fell into a silent room as only she occupied the entire upper floor since *Onkle* and *Aenti's* bedroom was on the first floor. From the open window, the rusty sound of crickets filled the summer night.

"Daniel has returned, *Gott*," she said into the stillness.

She swallowed, shifting bare knees on the hard, wood floor, drawing her nightgown snugly against her thighs. "I know I spoke with him when I shouldn't have. When he was shunned, but I realize now that I never loved him."

Hands gripping the fabric of gown, she leaned over the bed, "I have promised myself to Isaac, *Gott*. I do not know what I should do. I cannot marry Daniel, but he is back…and I never thought he'd return, particularly after having asked me to join him in the *Englischer* world. He looks so worn…so beaten."

Fervently, she bent forward, her eyes shut tight. "I'm here so far from my *Eldre*. I have no one to talk with, not really. No one to advise me."

She screwed up her face, eyes still shut tight. "*Onkle* doesn't think I should return to 'that *Schlang*', as he calls Daniel, but Bishop Fisher—who I've always trusted and respected—he acted as if I should return to Daniel."

Her head buried against the plain quilt on the narrow bedstead, she wept silently into the rough cotton, the warm moisture tracking down her cheek. "I am so tired, *Gott*. These past few months have been…so distressing and so confusing. Friends I never thought would turn their backs began whispering to each other about me. And yet you have directed us to forgive the trespasses against us."

Only peripherally conscious of the light breeze from the window that stirred wisps of her hair, she sniffed back at the tears clogging her nose now. "All the talk, the stares, *Gott*. It was all due to Daniel's having left and hints that maybe I had done something to drive him away."

Leaning against the bedframe, her sobs shuddered through her body, she pleaded for guidance. "What am I to do, *Gott*? Does forgiving Daniel's trespass mean my having to agree again to marry him? I don't know! And what of Isaac? How could I do this to him? Tell me, *Gott*. What do I do?"

Sobbing into the quilt top, the sharp scent of *Aenti's* homemade washing soap surrounding her, Mercy felt wracked with guilt and longing and sadness. She'd grown up with Daniel and he was now struggling in a way that could not but draw her compassion, even though she still felt angry with what he'd put her through. She knew now, though, that she didn't feel for him the love of a woman for a man.

A whispering thought came into her head. *Marry the one you love, Mercy. Marriage is a union for a lifetime. Marry the Mann you love.*

Struck, as if the words had appeared in her brain in flaming letters, Mercy lifted her head and stared blindly over the top of the bed. It was true. Marriage was a lifetime union, a joining in every endeavor. It should be founded in love. The kind of love she felt for Isaac.

Maybe… Maybe *Gott* had answered.

"Daniel!" Two days later, Mercy grabbed at the carriage frame next to her seat on the swaying driver's box. "Slow down, Daniel!"

She'd never have agreed to lunch with Bishop Fisher and Daniel at the Glick farm if she'd had any idea of this! At the time, her troubled heart had urged her to be kind...and she'd known Bishop Fisher her entire life.

Still!

With the buggy bouncing around as they thundered ahead of Isaac's, Mercy could only hold on for dear life. "Stop! Daniel, stop! Why did you speed up? Just because we happened to see Isaac? Stop!"

"He will see what kind of *Mann* I am," Daniel yelled out, his face contorting as he lashed at his buggy horse.

When she looked back through the jiggling buggy window, she could see Isaac's buggy sprinting after them.

With an excited flush on his cheeks and an almost fanatical gleam in his eye, Daniel yelled to her. "This Isaac needs to know I am not afraid to race his buggy!"

Closing her eyes against the sickening movement of the buggy as the countryside whipped past, Mercy prayed for *Gott* to save her.

At that moment, Isaac's buggy pulled alongside theirs, coming up fast from behind. When she agreed to lunch, she'd assumed she'd drive herself to the Glick house or walk. But when Daniel showed up just as she'd been walking to the barn to harness the horse, she'd never thought this would happen.

Daniel ignored Isaac as his buggy raced alongside theirs, not looking over to acknowledge his challenger.

This insane competition had sprung up as Daniel returned her back to *Onkle's* farm. They'd unexpectedly met Isaac's buggy at a crossroads and from that point, the race was on, Daniel having lashed his horse into jumping into a run and Isaac following.

Ignoring Isaac thundering next to the buggy they were in, Mercy leaned forward—still gripping the door frame beside her seat with the opposite hand—and tried to get Daniel to attend to her. She stretched her hand out to his arm. "Slow down, Daniel. This is not worth our lives."

He slanted a quick look at her before looking back at the road, raising again his whip. "He thinks he can beat me! I am not afraid!"

Recognizing that he was beyond hearing, she glanced over to where Isaac drove fast alongside them, his mouth set in a straight line. He flashed her a glance just then and almost in an instant of him looking her way—he had to have seen terror in her white face—she realized Isaac's buggy was slowing. Soon, he no longer raced next to them, his buggy dropping back to trail theirs. Apparently no longer feeling challenged by Isaac, who had clearly fallen behind them, Daniel also slowed. At a less terrifying speed, the buggies both trotted up to the Yoder farm.

Mercy took in a shaking breath, sending up a prayer of thanks.

"I have won. He must now see that he cannot beat me." Daniel said with a shaking, but satisfied voice. "We won!"

"Don't include me in that!" Mercy retorted angrily. She still remembered the grief when a neighbor's sons had died when racing. "How could you have endangered us like that?

He looked over, staring. "I had no choice. You have to see that."

Daniel's chest still rising and falling as he pulled his buggy up—horse trembling, it's flanks now flecked with foam—to a stop outside the farm house.

Mercy forced her fingers to uncramp from their grip, greatly comforted by the fact that Isaac still trotted his buggy behind them. Now that Daniel had stopped the buggy, she quickly clambered down from the buggy seat, saying in a shaking voice, "Goodbye, Daniel. Tell Bishop Fisher and *Frau* Glick again that I enjoyed lunching with them."

"When can I see you again?" Daniel asked quickly.

She stared at him. He had no recognition of having distressed her. Mercy pressed her lips together to keep a shaken—relieved—rebuke from bursting out of her.

Her side vision telling her that Isaac had parked his buggy nearby and was stalking toward them, Mercy was conscious of the thunderous scowl on his face. Not wanting this meeting to escalate into a brawl, she put up her hand to his chest as he came up to the buggy.

"You *Debiel*! You could have killed Mercy!!" Isaac thundered, his body tense beneath her palm.

"I wasn't the only moron racing," Daniel shot back defensively, glowering from inside the buggy.

"Yes," Isaac slipped his arm around Mercy and she leaned into him. "You were, you idiot! I only sped up after you because I saw your buggy flash past me and I thought the horse might have run away with you. I followed because I thought you needed help."

"Liar!" Daniel spat out the accusation. "You are a liar, Isaac Miller. You think I would let you win? Take your arm from around her! You saw I was with Mercy and you wanted to make me look bad!"

Mercy was conscious then of the house door opening as her *Onkle* came out on front porch. He stood there in his white shirt sleeves, his long beard seeming to bristle in anger.

Ignoring him, the two younger men continued to face off.

"You're not fit to drive a field cart!" Isaac didn't release her.

His face even redder, Daniel took a step closer to Isaac. "*Yah*? Well, I beat you, Isaac Miller, and Mercy wasn't in any danger!"

"You both could have been killed," Isaac retorted swiftly, "not that my concern is for your neck."

"Be quiet both of you!!" *Onkle* Yoder commanded. "And you, Mercy, come inside immediately. Now!"

"*Yah, Onkle*." Glancing up at Isaac, she smiled gratefully at him before slipping out of his embrace to head up the porch steps.

"And I don't care if you break your necks racing!" *Onkle* Yoder declared as he turned to follow her into the *Haus*, "Just as long as you leave my farm!"

"What are you doing here, Daniel?" Mercy stood at her *Aenti* and *Onkle's* open door later that evening, still annoyed by the escapade earlier.

"I must speak with you," he said abruptly, looking haggard and determined at the same time, no longer the cocky, outrageous *Mann* who'd tried to race Isaac. "Will you walk with me a little away from the *Haus*?"

He glanced over her shoulder to where she knew her *Onkle* and *Aenti* sat by the fireplace. "I think we should be...private."

As annoyed with him as she was for scaring her so and for blaming it all on Isaac, she still felt the tug of guilt at her reaction to the end of their marriage plans.

At the same time—after that morning—she wasn't going anywhere in a buggy with him.

"Just for a few moments," Daniel urged, his voice low. "We'll stay close. I really need to talk with you."

"Okay." She let the screened door close behind her, following him down the steps.

They walked toward her *Onkle's* orchard that was close to the house, stopping near an apple tree with immature fruit dangling from the branches. The smell of fertilizer was pungent and Mercy nervously brushed her hand against a walnut-sized apple.

"I don't know what there is to say, Daniel," she started. "I'm glad you have resumed a Godly life within the *Ordnung* rules, but I don't think—"

"Mercy!" he burst into speech. "I think you should know something about the *Mann* you've agreed to marry. This Isaac Miller."

Her words suspended by surprise, she looked at him with confusion.

His head dropped in contrition; Daniel briefly lifted his gaze to hers. "This is about me, as well. I—I didn't really tell you anything much when I ended our plans to marry and left for the *Englischer* world. I didn't say it, but—"

Waiting for him to continue, she finally said heavily, "*Neh.* You didn't tell me anything except that you weren't going to marry me and you were leaving to live as an *Englischer.*"

The weight and distress of that time seemed to rise up in her again. If it hadn't been for her having come here, she might still be in that mire. She'd made friends here and now that she was to marry and return here to live on his farm with Isaac, she could see herself happily making a life with him and with their children.

Above them, the apple tree boughs shifted a little in the breeze and the mottled shade moved over Daniel.

"I had questions then. Like many *youngies* do," Daniel admitted. "I've had them a while…like lots of others."

"But Daniel," she said in confusion, "you went on *rumspringa*. You returned to join the church. Didn't find your answers back then?"

"I came here for my *rumspringa.*" His admission was wrenched from him, made in a shamed voice. "I spent only two days in a big *Englischer* city. I was scared, though, and left to visit my *Onkle* Glick here."

Mercy stared. "Here? You came here? Okay, I can see how not having a full *rumspringa* might have left you still curious."

"But that wasn't why I didn't marry you and went into the *Englischer* world." Daniel spoke with a suppressed explosiveness that left her puzzled.

"Why did you then?" Standing here with him was so strange, so alien somehow. Even from this distance, she could smell the smoke in her *Onkle* and *Aenti's* fireplace.

"When I was here with my *Onkle* Glick, who was sick then, I worked in the fields with some other *Menner.*" Daniel turned to look at the tree trunk. "I was fine, Mercy. I was coming back to you, just as we'd planned. Until that Isaac Miller."

"Isaac? You knew Isaac? More than just meeting him? How could he make you not come home?" Mercy felt herself turning to stone. In all their conversations, Isaac had never mentioned having had any serious interaction with Daniel. He'd just said he met Daniel.

"*Yah*. I knew him. We worked the Glick fields together." Daniel looked at her steadily. "On that final day, he joked and sneered at me, Mercy. For running away from the *Englischer* world. He told me I wasn't a real *Mann*, that I didn't have the guts to make it there."

She felt her brows knit together in confusion. "Isaac? My Isaac?"

"*Yah*! This is why I'm talking about it now," Daniel said forcefully. "He dared me to prove myself in that world...and then when I went to stand up like a *Mann*, he stole my fiancée, Mercy. He stole you."

She put her hand to her head, shading her eyes briefly before dropping it back to her side. "He said that? That you could only prove yourself by leaving the church—leaving me—and moving to the *Englischer* world?"

Daniel responded after a moment. "*Yah*. What was I to do, Mercy? I'd already run scared from an *Englischer* town. I felt I had to—to prove myself."

"And Isaac pushed you into this?"

"I would not have gone if it were not for the things he said," Daniel insisted after a moment. "It was him! He played on my doubts—as small as they were at first—and scoffed at me. I had to go."

This last was said heavily, but Mercy wasn't listening anymore. She blinked several times, wrestling with a sense of unreality. This *Mann* she loved—he'd been behind the torment of the last few months? He'd caused her to be almost an outcast in her own church, so struggling as to leave her home town to come here for the summer? And he'd not told her of this?

"*Neh*, Daniel, not my Isaac," she said, still unable to abandon the Isaac she knew.

"*Yah*, it is just as I say, Mercy." Daniel possessed himself of both her hands. "You cannot marry him. Promise me that even if you no longer have room in your heart for me, you'll not marry Isaac Miller."

Mercy withdrew her hands from him, pressing them against cheeks that felt cold in the summer heat. "I must go, Daniel. I must go."

There was not a moment to spare. She had to hear Isaac's side of this.

"You told Daniel he didn't have the guts to live in the *Englischer* world? That he should leave to prove himself?" The questions burst out of Mercy's mouth in a furious stream, tears streaming down her face as she pulled her *Onkle's* buggy horse to a stop outside Isaac's barn.

The barn doors stood open in the summer evening and he moved to settle the two full milk pails he carried on a shelf near the barn door. Behind him, the cows in their stalls chewed the grain he'd left in their feeders.

"Mercy!" Isaac strode toward her buggy, hoping he had not heard her questions correctly. "Are you alright? I did not expect to see you this evening."

"*Neh*, I'm not alright." She ungracefully sniffled back her tears, glaring at him. "Why did you lie to me?"

"Let's tie up the horse over here at the post." Isaac tried a conciliatory smile. "We can go sit on the swing under my trees and talk."

Not moving her buggy, she gripped the reins tightly in her hands. "Did you? Did you dare Daniel to leave me? To prove himself in the *Englischer* world? How could you!?"

The torrent of words spilled from her. Isaac had never seen his beautiful Mercy so undone. A fresh wave of guilt crashed over him.

"I didn't!" he protested, feeling panicked. "I didn't dare him to leave you, Mercy. It wasn't like that."

Moisture still leaked from her angry blue eyes. "So you did know him? More than just meeting him? Daniel. You worked the Glick fields together. Yet you never told me of this, never said anything all the times you and I talked. Even when I spoke of having planned to marry him."

Feeling the rays of the setting summer sun on his bare head, Isaac stood dumb before her. He couldn't deny this. His sin had finally found him out.

"How…how do you know this?"

"Daniel! Daniel told me. You teased him and challenged him! And never said anything about it all this time. It was you. You pushed him into his flight!"

He swallowed then against the dryness in his throat. He loved her so much. Isaac sent up a prayer to *Gott* to help him, even though he knew he'd done wrong. It hadn't been intentional and he'd never planned any of this, but that didn't make him any less responsible for what he'd said. "*Neh*! Not pushed him!"

"But you knew him better than you said and you'd spoken to him of leaving? And yet you told me nothing! Even when I talked to you of my guilt!" She bent her golden head again, as fresh sobs broke from her.

"*Neh*, Mercy. It wasn't like that." Isaac's tongue finally loosened. "When I told you it wasn't your doing, it was because I knew. Not that I'd made Daniel do anything, but that I hadn't told you the full story. It was never your fault."

She stared at him, her eyes still stormy. "Why? Why didn't you tell me…? If you had nothing to hide."

He drew another deep breath. "I should have. I should have told you, but I didn't—"

"Why!? Why didn't you?"

"Because… Because it didn't seem necessary or…important. Until it was." Isaac took a step closer to her buggy. "I didn't say anything later…because I'd fallen—"

"No!" Her hands must have tightened on the reins, the horse picking up its head, ears shifting back. "No, don't say your silence was also my fault! You lied to me."

"Mercy." He grasped the buggy door. "I never meant to hurt you, believe me—"

"*Neh*!" She dragged a sleeve across her cheek and pulled it away, the fabric darker, damped by her tears. "I will not do this, Isaac Miller! I gave my heart to you as I never did to Daniel. And this is how you repay me!"

She must have yanked back on the reins, because the buggy horse shifted back then and Isaac stepped back.

"I will not do this! I cannot trust you!"

To his dismay, Mercy set the horse in motion and the buggy left his farm yard. For an insane moment, Isaac ran after her. He could jump on the buggy—maybe. In his mind, he envisioned leaping onto the back of her buggy and crawling forward along the side to wrest the reins from Mercy and stop the buggy.

Neh, he couldn't. Mercy would never forgive him. He didn't want to spook her or her horse.

Lurching to a stop, his chest heaving as he sucked in air, he watched her drive away. She'd be even angrier if he forced her to hear him. As if an angel of *Gott* placed a hand on his shoulder, he stood and watched her leave. His heart thundering in his chest, Isaac watched the buggy's pace quicken as it made the turn on to the main road. He'd never wanted to hurt Mercy. He loved her so much…and he'd wrecked everything.

CHAPTER TWELVE

"But he lied, Zacharius!" Mercy wiped away an angry tear two days later as she talked to the elderly *Mann*. After she'd given him the herbal mix and talked to him so frankly about Daniel, opening up to him about her distress now just seemed natural.

The old *Mann* twirled a stalk of little barley grass in his hand. "What did he lie about?"

The two sat on a hill in a field not far from her *Onkle's Haus*. The summer sun still shone on the tilled soil, but the breeze felt less heated, as if it knew fall was just around the corner.

"Isaac never told me he knew Daniel or that he was why Daniel left!"

"Was he? You know this?" The shade from Zacharius' straw hat shifted as he turned to look at her

"He admitted it! Well, he admitted he knew Daniel, that they'd worked side by side at the Glick farm before Daniel left for the *Englischer* world."

Old Zacharius' sigh was long and slow. "This end of your marriage plans with Daniel, it was hard on you."

"*Yah*. I lost many friends over it and—"

"Good friends?" Zacharius sent her a needle-sharp look.

She nodded slowly. "We'd...grown up together. We were *Maedels* together and learned all kinds of important things together."

Looking down to jerk at a piece of grass that grew in front of the log where she sat, Mercy went on. "Even the older members of the community treated me differently. You know how it is. *Eldre* that had all along been fearful their own children might leave the Godly life?"

"*Yah*." Her companion nodded. "It is often so. *Eldre* want heaven for their own. They want them to join the church and live right. It is natural."

"Well, even though I'd not left the church as Daniel did, I was stained by his having left me to join the *Englischer* world. As if I'd somehow driven him to it."

The old man snorted. "If you did, I don't have much of an opinion of his faith."

Mercy turned to look at him. "Why?"

Zacharius reached a gnarled hand to pat her knee. "What kind of a *Mann*, Mercy, lets another push him away from his faith?"

She wiped away another angry tear. "I don't know exactly what occurred between them, but shouldn't Isaac have told me he'd done more than met Daniel? And all this time, others have blamed me for Daniel leaving the church!"

The older *Mann* turned his straw-hatted head back to look out over the hill. "This choice had nothing to do with you and it was wrong for the *Eldre* of your community to hold it against you in any way."

"Thank you, Zacharius," she murmured, his comment settling into her thoughts like birds resting down on a pasture. "I feel better for having talked with you."

"*Gut*." He patted her awkwardly. "And you should let *Gott* help you sort all this through with Isaac."

She nodded slowly. "I will."

"I love her, *Daed*. I love her so." Isaac sat bare-headed on a nail barrel in Enoch's barn that same day, his hands dangling between his knees. Across the open space in front of the animal stalls, his *Bruder's* buggy was parked while Samuel and Enoch worked on a wheel they'd pulled off.

"And Mercy won't speak any further to you?" His shirt sleeve streaked with axel grease from wrestling with the wheel, Enoch knelt beside the buggy, looking over at Isaac.

"*Neh*," Isaac said heavily. "When I went to her *Onkle's Haus* this morning, Bishop Yoder put me off. He said Mercy wasn't there, that she would be out with her *Aenti* all day."

"Maybe she was out," Samuel held the wheel steady for Enoch, his needle-sharp gaze touching on his younger son.

"I don't think so." Isaac swallowed at the lump in his throat. "You know Bishop Yoder isn't the biggest fan of us Millers...but he seemed..."

"*Yah*?" From his spot kneeling beside the buggy, Enoch encouraged his brother to go on.

"He seemed almost as if he pitied me." Isaac flashed a look at his *Bruder* and *Daed*.

"Hello, Daniel Stoltzfus." Later that evening, Isaac spoke from the shadows clustering inside the Glick barn.

The other young *Mann's* head whipped around. "You!"

Isaac came forward to stand more fully in the light from a flickering lantern. "*Yah*, it's me."

Daniel turned back to the buggy horse he was leading from its stall, his face set.

"I know you have talked to Mercy, Daniel, but that is not why I'm here." Now that he faced the moment, Isaac felt lighter, no longer as burdened by his guilt.

Still yanking at the straps to harness the horse into the buggy shafts, Daniel snapped angrily, "Why are you here, then? I cannot talk. I must harness the buggy horse for my *Aenti*. Bishop Fisher and I go with her to eat with her friend."

"This will only take a moment." He looked down, gathering the words he knew he had to say. Squaring up to his own mistakes, Isaac said, "I need to apologize to you, Daniel."

"Apologize to me? Why? For stealing my girl?" Daniel wore his anger on his face, stiff and heated.

"*Neh.*" Isaac shook his head, his broad straw hat following his movement. "My sin took place before I met and fell in love with Mercy."

Glaring at him over the horse's back, Daniel ignored his mention of Mercy, snapping. "What do you mean?"

"Back when we first met on this farm, when your *Onkle* was ill, but still with us."

The other *Mann* said nothing.

"I sinned against you. I teased you and laughed at you after you talked of your farm. Of what an expert you were. I said you couldn't make it in the *Englischer* world." Isaac stopped, pausing before he went on. "You proved me wrong because you did survive in that world—after you left here. But if you're honest with yourself, Daniel Stoltzfus, I wasn't the only one sinning back before you left Mercy."

All Mercy could think as she sat at the Sunday meeting next to her *Aenti* was that she'd come here to Mannheim, to visit her *Onkle* and *Aenti* Yoder to get over the debacle with Daniel and now she was going home next week, more deeply in love, and more heart-broken, with Isaac Miller. In the front of the assembly, her *Onkle* Yoder was wrapping up his sermon. Another elder had spoken before him and while here Mercy had unconsciously memorized the rhythm of her *Onkle* Yoder's sermons. She could tell when he was finishing.

"God," her *Onkle* called out, "we pray for those who suffer senseless violence and injustice. We also pray that your goodness will have supremacy. We pray, too, for your blessing of mercy and grace and mercy on our troubled souls. In Jesus's name, Amen."

Mercy found herself silently mouthing the words along with her *Onkle*. She felt so broken inside—so grieved at Isaac's betrayal—that she could do now was pray for *Gott's* presence. This heartache didn't seem survivable.

"Now," her *Onkle* said, frowning from under bushy brows, "a member of our church wishes to confess before us, to repent of a sin against his brother."

Startled by the unusual and unexpected announcement, Mercy lifted her bent head. Next to her, *Aenti* Yoder sat placidly as if she'd known this was coming.

"He came to me and confessed his misdeed against his brother. Now he wishes to do so in front of this church."

There was a stirring in the seated group as members murmured and looked between themselves to see who would speak.

The sound of steady footsteps coming from the back of the room behind Mercy had her neck swiveling, as did everyone else's…and she felt her heart stop in her chest at the sight of Isaac approaching the front. Holding his hat in on hand, he stopped next to her *Onkle*.

To her shock, her *Onkle* placed his hand on Isaac's shoulder before speaking. "Isaac Miller has come to me and confessed to having heedlessly and thoughtlessly hurting another of our group."

Looking ahead, but apparently meeting no one's eyes, Isaac stood unmoving next to Bishop Yoder.

With her breath suspended in her chest, her heart beating painfully in her chest now, Mercy felt transfixed by the sight at the front. Surely, this could have nothing to do with her situation.

Bishop Yoder intoned. "Daniel Stoltzfus, please come forward to join us."

There was more whispering and stirring in the crowd at Daniel's name. Walking from the other side of the room—Bishop Fisher by his side—Daniel went to stand on the other side of *Onkle* Yoder.

Mercy had known her former fiancé was still here at his *Aenti* Glick's farm, but she'd had no contact with him since he'd come to tell her of Isaac's part in Daniel's leaving.

"Isaac Miller, speak your repentance." Her *Onkle* took a step back as did Bishop Fisher, leaving the two younger men facing one another in front of the group.

"I want to acknowledge—" Isaac paused to glance into the assembled church members, his gaze meeting Mercy's before he turned back to Daniel—"I acknowledge that I was wrong...and unkind in passing judgement on you when you came to work on your *Onkle's* farm last summer. If my unmindful and unkind words wounded you and contributed to your abandoning a life with *Gott*, I am deeply sorry. I was wrong to have spoken so. I should have kept my tongue more securely between my teeth. I confess to having unkind, ungodly thoughts and words with you. As I have repented to *Gott* and to the church, I ask also for your forgiveness."

Her heart in her throat, her breath suspended, Mercy felt her chin quivering as tears blurred her vision.

Around her, the congregation seemed also to hold its breath, transfixed by the real life drama unfolding in front of them. Mercy was aware that several heads turned her way, but she couldn't have stopped the tears that were now rolling down her face if she'd tried.

Through the wetness in her eyes, she saw that Isaac held his hand out to Daniel and that Daniel—hesitating for a moment— eventually shook it, not making any reply. Although this was probably the quickest handshake she'd ever seen, it was still amazing.

Mercy sniffed back the tears clogging her nose.

Isaac glanced at her *Onkle* and then back at the assembled group. "There is one other whom I have offended. One who was caused pain by the events of that day...and by my not confessing to it earlier."

Without even looking up, Mercy knew the heads of every adult in the congregation swiveled in her direction. She stared fiercely at her hands, clutched together in her lap.

She heard, however, Isaac's footsteps as he left the front where the bishops and Daniel still stood. At the end of the row of chairs, he stopped, "Mercy, I acknowledge my error…and ask you to forgive me."

Overcome, she could only mumble something incoherently, nodding several times. It wasn't the plain and simple way, to make a public spectacle of personal matters and she wasn't accustomed to this. Too much attention had come her way when Daniel jilted her.

To her embarrassed relief, her *Onkle* then drew all attention back to the front of the meeting as he began the service's final prayer.

Scuttling away after the service into the distraction of helping in the kitchen, she only thought of Isaac's confession when her mind wandered, which was too often, or when one of the women mentioned how brave he'd been and how handsome he'd looked— when making his confession. Working busily with the other women to feed everyone after the church service, Mercy chose to confine herself to kitchen work and let others serve the meals.

When she finally finished, she stepped out onto the back porch, straightening her black prayer *Kapp* and fanning her heated cheeks.

"Mercy Yoder."

To her shock, Isaac came forward from the shadow on the porch.

He reached out for her nerveless hand, "Mercy, I need to ask you again—this time with an untroubled heart. Will you still marry me?"

"It was very brave of you to stand before everyone like that Isaac." She lifted her face to look into his.

"I love you, Mercy. The very best thing that ever happened to me was when you asked me to pretend to court you."

Feeling herself start again to flush, she tried to pull her hand from his larger one.

"*Neh*," he said with a cheeky grin. "I have spoken to *Gott* and not only was I impressed to make an apology to Daniel and confess my part before the congregation, I was also convinced that you are the *Maedel* for me."

Suddenly the spring on the back screen door squeaked and when the sound drew her gaze, Mercy saw with a shock that Daniel had come out on the porch. She felt frozen and realized that Isaac, too, seemed startled, still holding her hand in his.

"I need to speak to you, Isaac Miller."

Although he'd put her through such turmoil, Mercy was struck by how firm and decided now were his words.

Next to her, Isaac nodded. "You are welcome to say whatever you need."

"When Bishop Fisher told me we were to both go to the front, I had no time to ask him why and so I was taken by surprise at your remarks in there." Daniel seemed to struggle with himself. "I didn't think fast enough to respond to you, but I need to tell you—here in front of *Gott* and Mercy—that yours alone were not all the mistakes of that day."

Mercy heard her own inward gasp and realized that she'd not often heard Daniel admit fault in anything.

"I was scared." A flush mantled his cheeks.

Despite the chattering of church members inside and around the house, their conversation felt very private. It was as if some invisible fence set them apart from the others.

"I ran. Ran from the *Englischer* world and—having come here to my *Onkle's* farm—I felt ashamed of my fear. That is why I bragged so that day, Isaac. Why I spoke of little else than the bragging I did that day we worked on the Glick farm." Daniel stopped, his expression seeming to harden.

Beside her, Isaac said nothing, seeming to realize that Daniel needed to speak. Mercy just looked at the *Mann* to whom she'd thought to pledge marriage, feeling little now except pity.

"That is also why I broke off our plans to wed, Mercy." Daniel looked over at her. "I wrongly felt I needed to leave to go back to the *Englischer* world to prove myself, but I ended our relationship to do that."

Mercy found her voice, realizing that all her resentment against Daniel—and her guilt over not missing him—had seeped away.

"That world is not harder," Isaac said finally. "It is just further from how *Gott* would have us live."

"I know that now," her former fiancé agreed. "I know, too, that I must live this life and that I will now be questioned. But this is the better life for me."

Daniel nodded, as if he was thankful to have made his apology. "That's all. Forgive me. I will leave you two in private."

He turned and went back inside, leaving them standing alone on the house's back porch.

Isaac tugged on her hand. "Mercy, will you still marry me? Please? I promise never to lie to you again…even by omission."

Having been staring at the spot Daniel had occupied, she turned back to look up again into Isaac's face. Zacharius's words suddenly rang in her head. It wasn't Isaac's fault that Daniel ran. *"What kind of a Mann, Mercy, lets another push him away from his faith?"*

Isaac pulled her back further into the porch shadow.

"I love you, Mercy. I should have told you about my conversation that day with Daniel. I needed to own up to it." He met her gaze. "As I said, I didn't think it was important to tell you at first. Then I was so afraid I'd lose you."

Flooded with a rush of love, she smiled up at him. "You were wonderful, telling the whole church about your guilt. It was brave of you and I thank you for that, Isaac."

"You haven't answered my question. Are you going to marry me, Mercy?" He took both her hands in his. "Tell me you'll work by my side until the end of our lives. Tell me you love me, still."

"I will marry you…and I will spend my life with you," she said, reaching up to meet his kiss.

Held tight in his embrace, she reflected briefly that *Gott* had led her to the right *Mann*.

After a moment, Isaac said, "I am more relieved than I can say, Mercy."

She took a deep sigh and snuggled against his embracing arms. "I have been so miserable, Isaac. More than ever before. I thought I'd been terribly mistaken in you. I am so glad this has not been true."

"As am I." He bent to press a tender kiss against her cheek. "I can no longer imagine a life without you as my *Frau*, Mercy. Can I take you back home to Elizabethtown to meet your *Eldre* and ask them if I can marry you?"

"You can," she responded, sending up a silent prayer of thanks to *Gott*.

Thanks so much for purchasing *Amish Princess!* If you enjoyed this book, please consider leaving a review on your favorite retailer, and look for *Amish Heartbreaker*, the next in the series!

Read on for a special look at the next in the series, Amish Heartbreakers!

AMISH HEARTBREAKER PREVIEW:

CHAPTER ONE

"But he lied, Zacharius!" Mercy wiped away an angry tear two days later as she talked to the elderly *Mann*. After she'd given him the herbal mix and talked to him so frankly about Daniel, opening up to him about her distress now just seemed natural.

The old *Mann* twirled a stalk of little barley grass in his hand. "What did he lie about?"

The two sat on a hill in a field not far from her *Onkle's Haus*. The summer sun still shone on the tilled soil, but the breeze felt less heated, as if it knew fall was just around the corner.

"Isaac never told me he knew Daniel or that he was why Daniel left!"

"Was he? You know this?" The shade from Zacharius' straw hat shifted as he turned to look at her

"He admitted it! Well, he admitted he knew Daniel, that they'd worked side by side at the Glick farm before Daniel left for the *Englischer* world."

Old Zacharius' sigh was long and slow. "This end of your marriage plans with Daniel, it was hard on you."

"*Yah*. I lost many friends over it and—"

"Good friends?" Zacharius sent her a needle-sharp look.

She nodded slowly. "We'd...grown up together. We were *Maedels* together and learned all kinds of important things together."

Looking down to jerk at a piece of grass that grew in front of the log where she sat, Mercy went on. "Even the older members of the community treated me differently. You know how it is. *Eldre* that had all along been fearful their own children might leave the Godly life?"

"*Yah.*" Her companion nodded. "It is often so. *Eldre* want heaven for their own. They want them to join the church and live right. It is natural."

"Well, even though I'd not left the church as Daniel did, I was stained by his having left me to join the *Englischer* world. As if I'd somehow driven him to it."

The old man snorted. "If you did, I don't have much of an opinion of his faith."

Mercy turned to look at him. "Why?"

Zacharius reached a gnarled hand to pat her knee. "What kind of a *Mann*, Mercy, lets another push him away from his faith?"

She wiped away another angry tear. "I don't know exactly what occurred between them, but shouldn't Isaac have told me he'd done more than met Daniel? And all this time, others have blamed me for Daniel leaving the church!"

The older *Mann* turned his straw-hatted head back to look out over the hill. "This choice had nothing to do with you and it was wrong for the *Eldre* of your community to hold it against you in any way."

"Thank you, Zacharius," she murmured, his comment settling into her thoughts like birds resting down on a pasture. "I feel better for having talked with you."

"*Gut.*" He patted her awkwardly. "And you should let *Gott* help you sort all this through with Isaac."

She nodded slowly. "I will."

"I love her, *Daed.* I love her so." Isaac sat bare-headed on a nail barrel in Enoch's barn that same day, his hands dangling between his knees. Across the open space in front of the animal stalls, his *Bruder's* buggy was parked while Samuel and Enoch worked on a wheel they'd pulled off.

"And Mercy won't speak any further to you?" His shirt sleeve streaked with axel grease from wrestling with the wheel, Enoch knelt beside the buggy, looking over at Isaac.

"*Neh,*" Isaac said heavily. "When I went to her *Onkle's Haus* this morning, Bishop Yoder put me off. He said Mercy wasn't there, that she would be out with her *Aenti* all day."

"Maybe she was out," Samuel held the wheel steady for Enoch, his needle-sharp gaze touching on his younger son.

"I don't think so." Isaac swallowed at the lump in his throat. "You know Bishop Yoder isn't the biggest fan of us Millers...but he seemed..."

"*Yah?*" From his spot kneeling beside the buggy, Enoch encouraged his brother to go on.

"He seemed almost as if he pitied me." Isaac flashed a look at his *Bruder* and *Daed.*

"Hello, Daniel Stoltzfus." Later that evening, Isaac spoke from the shadows clustering inside the Glick barn.

The other young *Mann's* head whipped around. "You!"

Isaac came forward to stand more fully in the light from a flickering lantern. "*Yah,* it's me."

Daniel turned back to the buggy horse he was leading from its stall, his face set.

"I know you have talked to Mercy, Daniel, but that is not why I'm here." Now that he faced the moment, Isaac felt lighter, no longer as burdened by his guilt.

Still yanking at the straps to harness the horse into the buggy shafts, Daniel snapped angrily, "Why are you here, then? I cannot talk. I must harness the buggy horse for my *Aenti.* Bishop Fisher and I go with her to eat with her friend."

"This will only take a moment." He looked down, gathering the words he knew he had to say. Squaring up to his own mistakes, Isaac said, "I need to apologize to you, Daniel."

"Apologize to me? Why? For stealing my girl?" Daniel wore his anger on his face, stiff and heated.

"*Neh*." Isaac shook his head, his broad straw hat following his movement. "My sin took place before I met and fell in love with Mercy."

Glaring at him over the horse's back, Daniel ignored his mention of Mercy, snapping. "What do you mean?"

"Back when we first met on this farm, when your *Onkle* was ill, but still with us."

The other *Mann* said nothing.

"I sinned against you. I teased you and laughed at you after you talked of your farm. Of what an expert you were. I said you couldn't make it in the *Englischer* world." Isaac stopped, pausing before he went on. "You proved me wrong because you did survive in that world—after you left here. But if you're honest with yourself, Daniel Stoltzfus, I wasn't the only one sinning back before you left Mercy."

All Mercy could think as she sat at the Sunday meeting next to her *Aenti* was that she'd come here to Mannheim, to visit her *Onkle* and *Aenti* Yoder to get over the debacle with Daniel and now she was going home next week, more deeply in love, and more heart-broken, with Isaac Miller. In the front of the assembly, her *Onkle* Yoder was wrapping up his sermon. Another elder had spoken before him and while here Mercy had unconsciously memorized the rhythm of her *Onkle* Yoder's sermons. She could tell when he was finishing.

"God," her *Onkle* called out, "we pray for those who suffer senseless violence and injustice. We also pray that your goodness

172

will have supremacy. We pray, too, for your blessing of mercy and grace and mercy on our troubled souls. In Jesus's name, Amen."

Mercy found herself silently mouthing the words along with her *Onkle*. She felt so broken inside—so grieved at Isaac's betrayal—that she could do now was pray for *Gott's* presence. This heartache didn't seem survivable.

"Now," her *Onkle* said, frowning from under bushy brows, "a member of our church wishes to confess before us, to repent of a sin against his brother."

Startled by the unusual and unexpected announcement, Mercy lifted her bent head. Next to her, *Aenti* Yoder sat placidly as if she'd known this was coming.

"He came to me and confessed his misdeed against his brother. Now he wishes to do so in front of this church."

There was a stirring in the seated group as members murmured and looked between themselves to see who would speak.

The sound of steady footsteps coming from the back of the room behind Mercy had her neck swiveling, as did everyone else's...and she felt her heart stop in her chest at the sight of Isaac approaching the front. Holding his hat in on hand, he stopped next to her *Onkle*.

To her shock, her *Onkle* placed his hand on Isaac's shoulder before speaking. "Isaac Miller has come to me and confessed to having heedlessly and thoughtlessly hurting another of our group."

Looking ahead, but apparently meeting no one's eyes, Isaac stood unmoving next to Bishop Yoder.

With her breath suspended in her chest, her heart beating painfully in her chest now, Mercy felt transfixed by the sight at the front. Surely, this could have nothing to do with her situation.

Bishop Yoder intoned. "Daniel Stoltzfus, please come forward to join us."

There was more whispering and stirring in the crowd at Daniel's name. Walking from the other side of the room—Bishop Fisher by his side—Daniel went to stand on the other side of *Onkle* Yoder.

Mercy had known her former fiancé was still here at his *Aenti* Glick's farm, but she'd had no contact with him since he'd come to tell her of Isaac's part in Daniel's leaving.

"Isaac Miller, speak your repentance." Her *Onkle* took a step back as did Bishop Fisher, leaving the two younger men facing one another in front of the group.

"I want to acknowledge—" Isaac paused to glance into the assembled church members, his gaze meeting Mercy's before he turned back to Daniel—"I acknowledge that I was wrong...and unkind in passing judgement on you when you came to work on your *Onkle's* farm last summer. If my unmindful and unkind words wounded you and contributed to your abandoning a life with *Gott*, I am deeply sorry. I was wrong to have spoken so. I should have kept my tongue more securely between my teeth. I confess to having unkind, ungodly thoughts and words with you. As I have repented to *Gott* and to the church, I ask also for your forgiveness."

Her heart in her throat, her breath suspended, Mercy felt her chin quivering as tears blurred her vision.

Around her, the congregation seemed also to hold its breath, transfixed by the real life drama unfolding in front of them. Mercy was aware that several heads turned her way, but she couldn't have stopped the tears that were now rolling down her face if she'd tried.

Through the wetness in her eyes, she saw that Isaac held his hand out to Daniel and that Daniel—hesitating for a moment—eventually shook it, not making any reply. Although this was probably the quickest handshake she'd ever seen, it was still amazing.

Mercy sniffed back the tears clogging her nose.

Isaac glanced at her *Onkle* and then back at the assembled group. "There is one other whom I have offended. One who was caused pain by the events of that day...and by my not confessing to it earlier."

Without even looking up, Mercy knew the heads of every adult in the congregation swiveled in her direction. She stared fiercely at her hands, clutched together in her lap.

She heard, however, Isaac's footsteps as he left the front where the bishops and Daniel still stood. At the end of the row of chairs, he stopped, "Mercy, I acknowledge my error...and ask you to forgive me."

Overcome, she could only mumble something incoherently, nodding several times. It wasn't the plain and simple way, to make a public spectacle of personal matters and she wasn't accustomed to this. Too much attention had come her way when Daniel jilted her.

To her embarrassed relief, her *Onkle* then drew all attention back to the front of the meeting as he began the service's final prayer.

Scuttling away after the service into the distraction of helping in the kitchen, she only thought of Isaac's confession when her mind wandered, which was too often, or when one of the women mentioned how brave he'd been and how handsome he'd looked— when making his confession. Working busily with the other women to feed everyone after the church service, Mercy chose to confine herself to kitchen work and let others serve the meals.

When she finally finished, she stepped out onto the back porch, straightening her black prayer *Kapp* and fanning her heated cheeks.

"Mercy Yoder."

To her shock, Isaac came forward from the shadow on the porch.

He reached out for her nerveless hand, "Mercy, I need to ask you again—this time with an untroubled heart. Will you still marry me?"

"It was very brave of you to stand before everyone like that Isaac." She lifted her face to look into his.

"I love you, Mercy. The very best thing that ever happened to me was when you asked me to pretend to court you."

Feeling herself start again to flush, she tried to pull her hand from his larger one.

"*Neh*," he said with a cheeky grin. "I have spoken to *Gott* and not only was I impressed to make an apology to Daniel and confess my part before the congregation, I was also convinced that you are the *Maedel* for me."

Suddenly the spring on the back screen door squeaked and when the sound drew her gaze, Mercy saw with a shock that Daniel had come out on the porch. She felt frozen and realized that Isaac, too, seemed startled, still holding her hand in his.

"I need to speak to you, Isaac Miller."

Although he'd put her through such turmoil, Mercy was struck by how firm and decided now were his words.

Next to her, Isaac nodded. "You are welcome to say whatever you need."

"When Bishop Fisher told me we were to both go to the front, I had no time to ask him why and so I was taken by surprise at your remarks in there." Daniel seemed to struggle with himself. "I didn't think fast enough to respond to you, but I need to tell you— here in front of *Gott* and Mercy—that yours alone were not all the mistakes of that day."

Mercy heard her own inward gasp and realized that she'd not often heard Daniel admit fault in anything.

"I was scared." A flush mantled his cheeks.

Despite the chattering of church members inside and around the house, their conversation felt very private. It was as if some invisible fence set them apart from the others.

"I ran. Ran from the *Englischer* world and—having come here to my *Onkle's* farm—I felt ashamed of my fear. That is why I bragged so that day, Isaac. Why I spoke of little else than the bragging I did that day we worked on the Glick farm." Daniel stopped, his expression seeming to harden.

Beside her, Isaac said nothing, seeming to realize that Daniel needed to speak. Mercy just looked at the *Mann* to whom she'd thought to pledge marriage, feeling little now except pity.

"That is also why I broke off our plans to wed, Mercy." Daniel looked over at her. "I wrongly felt I needed to leave to go back to the *Englischer* world to prove myself, but I ended our relationship to do that."

Mercy found her voice, realizing that all her resentment against Daniel—and her guilt over not missing him—had seeped away.

"That world is not harder," Isaac said finally. "It is just further from how *Gott* would have us live."

"I know that now," her former fiancé agreed. "I know, too, that I must live this life and that I will now be questioned. But this is the better life for me."

Daniel nodded, as if he was thankful to have made his apology. "That's all. Forgive me. I will leave you two in private."

He turned and went back inside, leaving them standing alone on the house's back porch.

Isaac tugged on her hand. "Mercy, will you still marry me? Please? I promise never to lie to you again...even by omission."

Having been staring at the spot Daniel had occupied, she turned back to look up again into Isaac's face. Zacharius's words suddenly rang in her head. It wasn't Isaac's fault that Daniel ran. *"What kind of a Mann, Mercy, lets another push him away from his faith?"*

Isaac pulled her back further into the porch shadow.

"I love you, Mercy. I should have told you about my conversation that day with Daniel. I needed to own up to it." He met her gaze. "As I said, I didn't think it was important to tell you at first. Then I was so afraid I'd lose you."

Flooded with a rush of love, she smiled up at him. "You were wonderful, telling the whole church about your guilt. It was brave of you and I thank you for that, Isaac."

"You haven't answered my question. Are you going to marry me, Mercy?" He took both her hands in his. "Tell me you'll work by my side until the end of our lives. Tell me you love me, still."

"I will marry you...and I will spend my life with you," she said, reaching up to meet his kiss.

Held tight in his embrace, she reflected briefly that *Gott* had led her to the right *Mann*.

After a moment, Isaac said, "I am more relieved than I can say, Mercy."

She took a deep sigh and snuggled against his embracing arms. "I have been so miserable, Isaac. More than ever before. I thought I'd been terribly mistaken in you. I am so glad this has not been true."

"As am I." He bent to press a tender kiss against her cheek. "I can no longer imagine a life without you as my *Frau*, Mercy. Can I take you back home to Elizabethtown to meet your *Eldre* and ask them if I can marry you?"

"You can," she responded, sending up a silent prayer of thanks to *Gott*.

Glossary of Amish Terms:

Aenti—Aunt
Bencil—silly child
Boppli—baby
Bruder—Brother
Daed—dad
Denki—Thank you
Debiel—moron
der Suh—my son
der Vedder—my father
Dochder—daughter
Eldre—parents
Englischer—non-Amish
Frau—wife
Geschwischder—brothers and sisters
Goedemorgen—good morning
Gott—God
Grossdaddi—grandfather
Grossmammi—Grandmother
Gut—good
Haus—house
Kapp—starched white cap all females wear
Lappich Buwe—silly boy
Liebling—sweetheart, darling, honey
Maedel—girl
Mamm—mom
Mann—man
Menner—Men
Narrish—crazy
Neh—No
Nibling—one's siblings children
Onkle—uncle
Ordnung—the collection of regulations that govern Amish practices and behavior within a district

Rumspringa—literally "running around", used in reference to the period when Amish youth are given more freedom so that they can make an informed decision about being baptized into the Amish church.

Schaviut—rascal

Schlang—snake

Scholar—young, school-aged person

Schweschder—sister

Verrickt—crazy

Wunderbarr—wonderful

Yah—yes

Youngies—adolescents. Young people.

About the Author

Author Biography:

Rose Doss is an award-winning romance author. She has written twenty-seven romance novels. Her books have won numerous awards, including a final in the prestigious Romance Writers of America Golden Heart Award.

A frequent speaker at writers' groups and conferences, she has taught workshops on characterization and, creating and resolving conflict. She works full time as a therapist.

Her husband and she married when she was only nineteen and he was barely twenty-one, proving that early marriage can make it, but only if you're really lucky and persistent. They went through college and grad school together. She not only loves him still, all these years later, she still likes him—which she says is sometimes harder. They have two funny, intelligent and highly accomplished daughters. Rose loves writing and hopes you enjoy reading her work.

Amish Romances:

Amish Renegade(Amish Vows, Bk 1)
Amish Princess(Amish Vows, Bk 2)
Amish Heartbreaker(Amish Vows, Bk 3)

www.rosedoss.com
www.twitter.com - carolrose@carolrosebooks
https://www.facebook.com/carol.rose.author

Made in the USA
Columbia, SC
11 January 2019